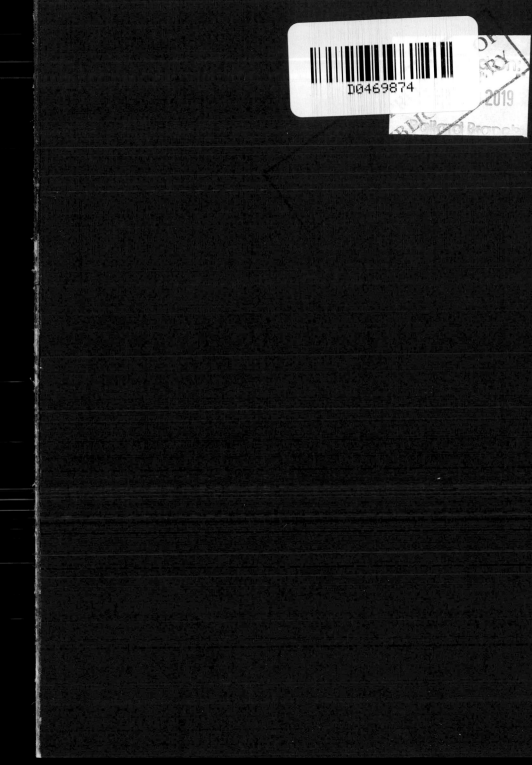

THE BIG IMPOSSIBLE

THE BIG IMPOSSIBLE

Edward J. Delaney

TURTLE POINT PRESS *Brooklyn, New York*

Requests for permission to make copies of any part of the work should be sent to: Turtle Point Press, 208 Java Street, Fifth Floor, Brooklyn, NY 11222 info@turtlepointpress.com

Library of Congress Cataloging-in-Publication Data

Names: Delaney, Edward J., 1957– author.
Title: The big impossible : novellas + stories / Edward J. Delaney.
Description: Brooklyn, NY : Turtle Point Press, 2019
Identifiers: LCCN 2019013787 (print) | LCCN 2019017097 (ebook)
ISBN 9781885983756 (ebook) | ISBN 9781885983749 (pbk. : alk. paper)
Classification: LCC PS3554.E436 (ebook) | LCC PS3554.E436 A6 2019 (print)
DDC 813/.54—dc23
LC record available at https://lccn.loc.gov/2019013787

The following stories appeared previously in the following publications: "Clean" in *The Atlantic*, "Medicine" in *The Alaska Quarterly Review*, "Grassfire" in *The High Plains Literary Quarterly*, "My Name Is Percy Atkins" in *West Branch*, and "Buried Men" in *The Ontario Review*.

Design by Alban Fischer Design

Printed in the United States of America

CONTENTS

PART ONE

Clean

You think of that night endlessly from your imprisonment, the decisions made, the chain of mistakes. It had begun with your two buddies, a quart of cheap vodka and a half-gallon of orange juice; one of these friends had suggested the confrontation. Said this kid, Barry, was cutting in on your girl—well, she wasn't even really your girl yet; the flirtation was just in its formative moments—was something that you, at sixteen, had no intention of allowing.

He'd been walking home, at night. He worked at a burger place in that little scrub-oak town out near the Cape Cod Canal and, even drunk, you'd known a spot to intercept him. Again, at the suggestion of your friends. There he was, his backpack slung on his shoulder, looking at you as if he's not even sure who you were. You'd decided you would rough him up, and he decided to fight back, and you'd picked up a rock, and you'd swung it at his head. A minute later he was on the ground, dead.

You think of how, as drunk as you had been, you instantly sobered. The discussion was quick, and its determinations would last for a lifetime. You waited for him to somehow come to; soon enough he was irredeemably cold. But you three had decided by then. No one would tell. No one would try to explain that the moment was one of passion and mistakes. In your long memory, telling wasn't even part of that shaky conversation, your voices all gone weepy and scared.

You took the rock, with its rime of blood, and threw it in a pond. You filled Barry's backpack with other rocks and into the pond that went, too. You were driving your old Pontiac, and the first odd decision was to drive home, go in your bedroom, strip the top sheet off your bed, and bring it back to the scene as your buddies waited, hidden in the nearby woods with Barry, the body dragged in by the feet. You got your mother's gardening trowel from the nail in the garage. Then her garden claw.

By the time you drove up, watching for headlights, you had calmed a bit. You were thinking now, your head clicking with logic and forethought that was a revelation in itself. Your buddies had kicked the blood under dirt and you wondered as you came back if they had been talking of turning you in. Apparently, they had not.

The body was wrapped in the sheet and you drove to a place you thought would work. Again, the choices made: A place close to your house, less than a half-mile, too easy. But a place far enough away from other houses and with somewhat yielding ground. Three of you, all high-school athletes, did not tire that night, rotating through the clawing and digging, going deeper, no sloppy shallow graves here. When his sheet-wrapped body went into the groundwater that had gathered at the bottom, it felt for that glorious instant as if the problem was now solved. You all filled the hole with dirt and stomped it down, then drove to the ocean at dawn and walked into the surf, fully clothed, emerging salty and bloodless.

This was '72. You think of forty years gone past, and the girl. For days after, you did the calculus, of risk and probability. You realized in that panicky first day that his wallet went into the ground with him; everything had not been fully considered. You and the other two never spoke of it directly again, and you weighed the human factors you could not control. You sensed, by the light of day, some shrill and growing prospect of being caught. Then, you got lucky. Barry, an aspiring hippie, had been trying to get your girl to take off with him, hitchhiking with backpacks, cross-country. He did not get along with his parents; he craved adventure and escape. She told the police she guessed he must have gone, and then she keened at her presumed abandonment. You heard about that at school and felt a surge of both relief and fury, that Barry had made the plan and that she had apparently considered it. You hated her for choosing him.

The conclusion was simple. Barry was deemed just another wandering soul, a longhair, a dreamer. He'd return in due time. The only thing was that your mother could not stop going on about the missing bedsheet. Where did it go? How do you lose a bedsheet? "Now you've broken up the set," she said. You heard her telling the neighbor about her son mysteriously losing a sheet, and you wanted to make her stop.

The girl: Barry gone, you dated her for a few months but found you had nothing to talk about. She turned out, in fact, to be mildly irritating, and that was that.

Senior year: Thinking back over the years, you are appalled to consider how little you worried about what had happened. In fact, you barely thought about it at all. In your mind, *it* (you could not bring yourself to use the more specific word) wasn't even your fault: You'd been egged on, drunk, by the other two. You met other girls, and you played your games, and you avoided the vicinity of the grave. You were an adolescent who did not dwell on things that might ruin your fun. Your decisions came from that, and you surprised your parents by going to college very far away.

Your buddies: You realized that they would not talk, even when drunk. Besides, the three of you were no longer that friendly. Typical teenagers, you all had found other interests, other friends.

Those were the years when you needed to tell yourself what you were, and what you were not. So: You were a good person. You were not violent. Indeed, in those years you became milder and milder, almost as if shedding the ill-thought fashions of your youth like a bad sweater. Changing times. You held that memory in your stomach, but you functioned, actually, *well*. It had been three years then, and no one was going to find out. Then you went home for Thanksgiving. Your little Massachusetts town was spreading itself out, and you saw bulldozers edged up toward that once-remote place in the woods. A new housing tract. You spent the weekend sleepless, telling yourself that even when the body emerged, the police would have no suspects, no motive. But the soft ground in which your secret lay was wetland. New environmental laws had been passed, and the housing tract stopped less than a hundred yards from where the body lay buried. The next spring, you told your parents you were going to stay on at your distant school, do summer classes, accelerate, and when you were done with that you stayed on as a grad student. When those unbidden memories occurred, those pre-dawn panics, you pushed deeper into your studies, forcing the ghosts away. You graduated with your parents and sisters smiling at your side for the picture, and then you moved farther west.

In love, you married. Some nights you felt so intimate with her you wanted to tell her, felt you had to. Felt she would hold your secret and love you still. But then one odd night, an awkward dinner, and you weren't so sure you two were always in tune. The marriage evened into something mellow and a bit more distant, and the impulse passed. When you had children, you tried to be good. The business flourished, and the money came in without much struggle.

Why, in your late thirties, did the hidden crime begin to obsess you? When you began to read the articles about DNA, and how it could tell of a long-past crime, did you begin to see a story that hadn't been completely written? You became an insomniac. You played that one minute of your life in an endless loop on the pale wall of your skull. The phone felt suddenly as if it would go off. You would see a police car two thousand miles from your hometown and feel an edge. You felt in those years as if your unmasking was imminent, but then nothing happened. During the holidays, you had your parents out for a visit to a warmer climate. Sometimes, your mother would start in about the missing sheet. You'd all laugh in reminiscence.

Your father died, and you flew back to take care of things. You went through his desk, sorting out his papers, tending to your mother. At the bottom of a drawer was a yellowed bit of newspaper, clipped down to a tiny headline and one-paragraph item. "Local Boy Reported Missing." Strangely, the photo in the paper, though blurred, didn't match the memory in your head, of that face on the side of the road, turning to meet the judgment of your headlights.

Why had your father kept this? What did he guess? Did you make noise that night as you came and went? At the funeral, a Navy ensign played taps, and your mother got the triangled flag. Your father went into that neat, nearly surgically cut hole with his own secrets. You burned the newspaper in his kettle grill on the back deck, kindling some charcoal and then making a steak.

That evening, you left your mother's house near dark and went walking in those woods. Twenty years had passed, more. You'd built a life now. In this cold ground was what would always threaten to change it. You had an exact memory of the spot he was buried, but that memory failed you, too. You could find no place that was at all like the place you remembered.

Flying home, you realized someone had to have been following all this. Were the police so sure of the hitchhiking story, even in 1972? Could they not have tried to look into it? Who was assigned the case, and could he have known of you? But you saw no signs of any investigation. Maybe when Barry eventually did not return home, too much time had passed. Maybe they just didn't care that much. But you knew a file must have been kept at the police station, and your desire to open that file and see what was written became instantly unbearable. But you were 35,000 feet in the air, over the arrayed pivot-circles of Kansas, heading toward the sun. By the time you landed, you felt the anxiety was finally over. In long-term parking, you slipped into the leather seat of your German car as if it was a glove that fit you perfectly.

In your forties, you thought of the boy less, but when the memory came to you it gave you an unremitting ache. You could barely remember who you were then, what urges drove you, or what aspirations you'd had. The indisputable irony was that the aftermath of all that had given you focus, and direction. Who would you have become instead, if It had not happened? You also felt a welling anger at Barry himself. If he was going to leave, why did he not just leave? Was this talk of hitchhiking just something to woo his wanted girl, or was he really going to do it? You thought about how, if he'd decamped a day sooner, or if you three had not drunk that plastic jug of orange juice and that bottle of vodka, that night would just be something forgotten, rather than a specific date on the calendar you suffered through each year, and by which you could count, to the very minute, your growing remove. The colors faded like a washed-out Kodachrome.

In the eleventh year of your marriage you found out your wife had been having an affair. She confessed; you were shocked. Boredom, she told you tearfully. Someone else had offered escape, she said.

"I love you," she said, "but you're a dull, passionless person. You have no fire."

She was right, but now wrong. You knew who the man was. For the first time in thirty years, the familiar urge came back to you, for the same reasons. The careful decades of telling yourself you were different now crumbled, instantly. You could have done it again, right then, had you decided to. But you did not.

Instead you got up from the couch and went out on your deck with a drink (good wine, never the hard stuff) and looked at the sky and thought about the careful, boring man you had sculpted yourself into. No passion at all. Later, your tear-stained wife came out and sat with you in the wind of sunset and said she wanted to try to work things out, for your daughters. Her love of your daughters made her want to stay with you and find the middle ground. And you both did. You wanted badly to offer your forgiveness, as you badly wanted forgiveness for yourself.

Yes, you'd had chances for affairs, but had always held back. Your reason wasn't strict morality, more the fear of the weight of yet another secret. The thought of that was just too heavy. You accepted life as it was, and you walked in the evening to get air.

One night, a few years later, the phone rang and your wife held it in front of you saying, "It's Dennis." Dennis who? You heard the voice and instantly you were back to that night. Dennis, your long-ago buddy, was not well. Lymphoma. Three or four months. He had the urge to tell, to unburden. He had thought about that night every day of his life, he said into the phone. He'd spoken of it many times over the years, he said, in the darkness of the confessional. Father Shea had told him his soul was now clean, even as it felt not.

"Dennis, I can't tell you what to do," you said to him. "We're all different people now. Do what you feel you must. I would understand."

"Thank you for that," he said. "I guess telling would be easy for me now. I'll be dead before I have to face the consequences. But I think we all should have." You had the phone to your ear, listening to him. You were two strangers. As Barry had been. Someone about whom you knew nothing.

Dennis asked about your family then, and you told him. He said he had not heard from Jeff in years, no idea where he'd gone. When you hung up, you were giddy that the secret might come out. You were surprised, and gratified, at the relief you felt. For weeks you sat at your desk and prepared things, just in case. You slept straight through each night. You got on the computer and read about juvenile law. You were all sixteen when it happened. Had the three of you gone to the police that night, explained you'd been in a fight that went out of control, you would have been out by the age of eighteen. Now you quietly imagined the neat rectangle of a cell, with a thin mattress. The thought didn't seem as foreboding as it had when you were young and felt the possibilities of life. This future now seemed orderly, calm. You had forgiven your wife, and you imagined and nearly craved her own understanding. You had never given her the opportunity, never shared the secret. You concluded that was why, in your entire life, you'd never felt true intimacy.

That night, you Googled Barry's name and found nothing. So many years had passed; who'd remember? Where would Barry's name have been preserved? He seemed to have never existed. You remembered back in '75, when word had quietly come that his parents had moved away, some new job or escape from worries. But now, so long after, people would remember him. You lay down in bed against your sleeping wife and felt the powerful promise of the simplicity, and the real facts of your life.

But your conversation had apparently given Dennis the

peace not to speak, or perhaps he had simply died before he had a chance. No one told you anything. After a long stretch of months in which a tap did not come to your door, you went to the online obituaries and saw that he was gone. You checked on Father Shea, and he too had passed years before. Your younger daughter walked in the room, said you looked weird, and walked out. By dinner, you were who you were again.

Later on that year, your mother succumbed, the story of the missing bedsheet forever silenced. Back in town to close the house, you now did not venture into the dark woods. You and your sisters sorted things out and renewed bonds. You promised to stay in touch, knowing you probably would not.

That evening, at a hotel by the airport, you watched local TV. To your shock, you saw a vaguely familiar face. A woman, real estate. She was the girl, from all those years before. You'd nearly forgotten her name. She was, like you, an aging person. Now she sold high-end real estate and seemed to have had at least some ineffectual cosmetic surgery. She had a horsey, drawn face, and wore a giant rock on her left ring finger. Did she ever think of Barry? He'd only been a boy who made her promises then went off hitchhiking, leaving her out of his adventure. You wondered about it as you tried to sleep.

You flew home and idly considered the third of you, Jeff, somewhere out there with the other half of your secret, the last person with the power to tell. You sat on your deck and drank some wine and watched the sunset over the Pacific. Another day elapsed between you and that night. You had come to this place, imprisoned by what you were, what you had done, never able fully to be inside the life you made. You imagined how you would feel to just live.

The irony of getting away with something was that you were your own keeper. You were the executioner: In a pang of remorse you could just open your mouth and change your life. You felt almost as if you would. But, greedy, you always wanted to savor one more day, even as that day turned leaden with a memory that no longer went away. It could not be put aside as it was your senior year of high school, when something that had happened six months before may as well have never happened at all. Who were you? How did you find the way to make it just not be? Now, an older man, you decided that if the time came, to tell, you would edit Dennis and Jeff from the story, a small act of charity.

The vast ocean shimmered below you, endless expanses in which things could be effortlessly hidden, even as what you looked at was only a knife's edge to the greater stretches past the distant horizon. Even as the silver surface only whispered of the dark depths, the things you could not see. This was your life now, orderly, calm. This was how things were now. Clean. You knew you would sleep as well as one might be expected to, all of us with our own given histories.

My Name Is Percy Atkins

1. A more immediate observation of a vintage wallflower

The air-conditioning is already getting a bit dodgy. On this fall evening, 1968, Tampa, in the clubhouse of the Ocean Breeze Apartment Community, the air comes out leaden and sweaty, and Percy needs to take purposeful and conscious breaths, deep down. The perfume is absolutely bloody stifling, too many florid old ladies packed into too small a space.

He stands at the edges of it all, where the checkerboard linoleum meets the woodgrain paneling, where the metal folding chairs are placed with liberal room in between for the wheel-chair people, where everyone is old and where he may be the last one who still feels the same boyish anxiety that goes with the thought of actually approaching a female, even at a retire-ment-community square dance.

He wears a tag that is pinned to his shirt, over the heart. The tag already has the MY NAME IS . . . printed on it, and the community center calligraphy class has filled in the name in flamboyant hand: Percy Atkins. He is dressed in a cowboy shirt (white yoke over salmon body, no fringes but pearl-like snap buttons, bolo tie with a turquoise setting, chinos, slip-on deck shoes, and a straw cowboy hat with a red trim, something the dime-store cashier might have thought he was buying for a grandchild. He has no grandchildren or children, and he has lived in Ocean Breeze for only a few months. He's been in Tampa for nearly ten years. He was widowed not even a year ago and he had finally decided he could not bear the house alone. Now he's damned near afraid to go out.

Ocean Breeze is made up of the central clubhouse/pool complex, from which six long buildings radiate like spokes, each of those spokes a train-like procession of small efficiency apartments, a blacktop parking lot out beyond, encircling the place like the tire on the wheel. He has mostly stayed inside since arriving here. Early in the mornings, he drives in his Buick Special to his old neighborhood, where he can walk the familiar streets and then onto the nearby city golf course, where he is not an unfamiliar figure, where he will not be asked to leave, and where the occasional errant shot bouncing toward him helps him know he can move lightly when he must.

He is a compact man, and lean, the waist still at twenty-eight inches but the chest much shrunken from what it was in his working days. He's lived in the States for more than fifty years. He's taken an American wife and now he's buried her, and what were once yearly trips back to England (all-night train to New York and a Cunard liner across) having first been infrequent and then not at all as Martha became more unsteady.

Percy Atkins coughs, thinking about that. About him, of all people, surviving his wife. That one was a complete surprise. He never thought he'd be approaching something, in his dotage, resembling dating.

2. Various recollected unpleasantnesses, often repeated

1916: The smell of the dank wool is the most curious connection to home. His whole life, that wet musky scent that is walking in the Sheffield rain, on muddy roads; the smell of horse and ale and hay; the smell of sodden childhood. His boots sink to the ankles and he slogs on, shivering, the skin taut beneath the wool underwear and wool uniform and rucksack. This is the farthest end of the world for a boy from Britain: France. The oozing roads, the fulsome language he cannot disentangle. The puzzle of the terrain on which his column marches, heading for the front alongside a convoy of lorries.

He volunteered for this, as all the boys of his neighborhood, the "Pals" who have been called upon by Lord Kitchener to serve. His unit, the 2nd Barnsley Pals, have fallen in behind the Accrington Pals, with the Fusiliers ahead of them. There is a sense of giddiness in them all, the kind of laughing and sarcasm that is easy to boys who know each other well, the long tedium of the march being broken up by the transmuting cliques and rivalries, the idle boasts and challenges to same. Much seems to revolve around arm wrestling or drinking contests. They've carried many of the old grudges all the way to the front—the competed-for girls, the lost football games, the schoolyard fights. Percy can't get comfortable. He is not one to be chatty in any event.

June and the rains are unceasing. They march with long woolen coats on, making the day all the more stifling. They will make camp in late afternoon, and they will sit as the smell of the stew begins to waft across the cheerless fields. They will play cards and write letters.

The lice embed in the skull, the skin is unwashed for many days' time, his wispy beard itching under the helmet strap, and the stomach aching for more than what is given after a day's march with a four-stone pack. But who is he to complain? Everybody's putting up with it.

3. Sad revelations acknowledged at a certain point in one's life

There is never enough money, and likewise never enough room. It is 1938 and he has turned forty and they still live in that third-floor apartment up under the eaves in Fall River, Massachusetts. He is careful with their money. There is a Depression on. Most of his mild wealth is in cash, in rubber-banded stacks in the heavy iron safe in the corner of the bedroom. The quote-unquote nest egg. The quote-unquote Family Fund. He has forbidden her from knowing the contents of their worth. She is not privy to the safe's combination.

He is past forty and she's just a bit younger. They remain up under the eaves waiting for something to happen. But there will be no discussion of the fact that nothing has happened, nor likely will happen. He comes home from the mill and sits in his chair and reads the evening newspaper, and after dinner they might listen to the radio. At night she sleeps as his coughs rumble up, up from other lives, but never extinguished, one guttural hack that arcs through the entirety of adult life.

Tonight is like all the others. They've just eaten dinner and he has settled into his overstuffed chair, that one prized possession, to read his evening paper. He keeps up with the troubles on the other side, this growing new war. It is stunning that this is to be. The memory of the Great War is an unshakable constancy for him, descending in his dreams or simply as a thought that rides on with him, like clouds in the sky of his life. This Depression keeps one's ruminations more immediate. Everyone is struggling.

He is in the middle of his life and he has felt its long skein of easy concession. Even in the twenties, when others were doing well, he was only finding his way, first to Toronto, where the Canadian veterans had no work, then to Massachusetts, to the mill. When most of those others were brought down by the Crash, his only consolation was that he didn't have too far to fall. When he and Martha now find themselves childless in middle age, they are neither fully surprised nor disappointed.

"We probably didn't have the money for it," Martha says.

"Probably not," he says.

"We have our life . . . this one," she says, and he can only nod.

"It's not your fault," she says, and he doesn't nod at all.

4. The suggestion of a mild but potentially troublesome situation

The outer edges of the clubhouse recreation room are mostly peopled by the infirm and truly aged, not the healthy aged. It is a fact of this generation and also of medicine that Percy Atkins is one of a very small number of ambulant, lucid men in this "community," while conversely there seem to be untold numbers of preternaturally healthy female septuagenarians who barrel around the place with the kind of energy that sends unceasing loads of brownies north to grandchildren and keep the gardens of Ocean Breeze so perfect the flowers have begun to look artificial. They all say "Hi!"—that big American "hi" he hasn't completely gotten used to in all these years. They have sun-splotched, lined faces under whimsical sunbonnets and hair hued as idiosyncratically as their beloved varietals, any color you want, any version. They chatter from the lawn chairs that they cluster along the covered breezeway leading from each front door to the scorching parking lot with its sponge-like asphalt. They retreat after lunch to their blasting televisions and their histrionic "stories" that blare multiphonically from open windows. They seem not to need air-conditioning even in the stoutest heat, while he and the other old men seem never to turn off their wheezing, window-mounted units.

And they are all here now, these women. In fact, at this moment, they are for the most part dancing with each other. The square dancing itself has not yet commenced, so the ladies are dancing in couples to the prefatory polka that issues from the record player in the corner, attended to by Staff. Staff is an assortment of tanned women in their late thirties who appear in the morning hours to be sure that if one is eager to paint, exercise, discuss great books, create floral arrangements, or write in calligraphic form, that one may most certainly do so. Most of them seem to be named Eileen or Nancy, most likely the most popular baby-girl names of the late 1920s, but they must be differentiated as they come and go, leading to such coinages as "The New Eileen" or "Blond Nancy." Most of Staff will answer cheerfully to either of the names, even if they are not even one of those. Staff will likewise remember your name without fail. *Hi, Percy!*

The women dance on. No men have yot entered the fray. Most sit in chairs at the edges with their lemonades and ginger snaps, lost in themselves, leaning on their canes, even in their cowboy garb. Many profess to be here only as spectators. Staff has decided that Women dancing as Men will wear yellow roses. Staff has thoughtfully provided for the event.

Off toward the main entrance to the recreation room is Mrs. Gottlieb, who seems to have positioned herself strategically so as to be the first to greet all arriving guests. Mrs. Gottlieb is exceptionally friendly, in mufti with a billowing dress that, while quite loose, further advertises the sheer mass of the woman. Her makeup, as is the case with most of the women, is primarily a crimson lipstick that breaches the borders of the lips themselves and will be applied and re-applied as the festivities continue.

He looks around the room, and as he does his tongue works itself along the edges of his dental plate, a nervous gesture. How old he has become. He has come to realize in late age that old women aren't any more attractive to him than they were when he was younger, and the converse must most certainly be true. He is fit, all things considered, but he is an elderly man, white hair cut close along cracked and sun-leathered skin. *We all just want a bit of respite from the solitude.* Who is he to be picky? But as Mrs. Gottlieb turns and her glance catches him looking, she smiles coquettishly.

She lives in the next spoke over in their wheel, in Cluster 3, and she loves to wave. She's always standing up from her gardening and waving, in big arcing arm motions that worry her aging flesh, waving as he walks to his car in the early-morning cool, waving as he returns. *Hi, Percy!* His return wave has consequently been a more tentative one, mostly in the wrist.

5. The regrettable moment in which things must be ventured

Dawn. Through the buildup, the bombardment of the Germans has been relentless. It is a gray and sticky day in which the uniform, soaked through from the previous days' heavy rains, barely lets him move. His boots sink in the mud of the trench floor, oozed up over the duckboards, and all along the way there are boys crouched over their rifles, waiting the order to go over the top.

Percy is huddled in the trench next to his chum from home, Wesley Hitchens. They have been together since induction, two former schoolmates who didn't know each other very well. Wesley is terrified, while Percy has simply become disconnected from it all, has somehow been able to blot from his mind the idea that there is any outcome to the actions they take. His consciousness refuses to ride ahead of the moment at hand. Years later, he will recognize that the courageous one of them was Wesley, brave enough at least to take each action with full knowledge of his remote chances. Percy will recognize he had simply run away in the only way that he could.

They have been here a long time and life down in the ground makes each hour and day crawl by with brutal exactitude. Percy is nineteen, Wesley eighteen, and they've found an affinity that traces itself back to nothing more complicated than their bottomless preoccupation with card games. Whist, in particular. They are forever hunting for thirds and fourths when they can be off-duty in their funk holes cut into the sides of the trenches, and from time to time, some of the Highlanders Regiment clamber down the boards in their kilts and tam o' shanters to join a game and try to steal away some biscuits or a tin of marmalade. Beyond, the earth is turned and cratered, the trees are stripped of their leaves, the only birds they see in the sky are the lurching homing pigeons, in their low trajectories, carrying messages on their legs.

The word has circulated down the way: When the order comes, they are to climb the steps that have been shovel-carved into the front of the trench and begin advancing, shoulder to shoulder. They have on their fifty-five-pound packs, all the equipment they will need to set up in forward positions.

"Last time in this bloody trench," Wesley whispers, his voice quavering.

"Indeed."

"I hope they find higher ground for us to dig the next one."

"I suppose," Percy says, for it is he who is not keen on the idea of getting out of this trench, despite its fetid mud, its stink, and its complement of slithering rats.

Now they hear the relayed shouts from down the line, and they begin to clamber up. It's a cool morning, and the sun is just beginning to peek through after so many days of rain. They have been told that the bombardment of the last three days has all but wiped out the Germans. They are to now take that easy ground. Percy is bracing himself for the sight of the mangled remains, the silent witness of the enemy bodies. The general mood, however, is of relief. Far down the way, one of the brigades has a football, that they kick out ahead of them, the ball bouncing ahead and coming to rest to wait for them. Boys move forward, working through their own defensive wires with long-handled cutters, through to open ground. Percy has his gun barrel forward. He grasps the otherworldliness of being up on the top, moving without constriction, regarding the world from its surface rather than from its gashed insides. He feels the momentary sensation of being unbound. And when the machine-gun fire opens up from the other side, from the trenches that they have been told will be full of dead men, he is almost unable to understand.

Men are being hit all around him, instantaneously, and he goes down, the great pack slamming on top of him as if in emphasis. The machine-gun fire is hard and steady, and he can hear the bullets humming just above him. Ahead, the front lines have been brought down completely. The ones of them still alive are trying to drag themselves back. His own face pressing the mud, he still sees their wild eyes. If there is shouting, it does not register. A shell comes down not twenty feet from him, but it makes a weak bang—a seeming dud, no concussion, no hail of dirt or hot shrapnel. He is completely frozen in his indecision. To turn back, unwounded, will have consequences; he's heard no order to pull back and to do so on one's own is to return to a firing squad. But ahead, the bodies are toppled like a long chain. He watches the wounded, coming back, crawling, terrified. Everyone is shouting, but he understands none of it. He turns to locate Wesley, but he cannot make out any shape in the suddenly rising fog. And it is only then that he realizes he is enveloped in the gas.

6. The thing in which one finds some long-embedded fact

At his mid-fifties, his breathing has become the metronomic, a register above unconscious effort. The lungs, shrunken by the gas to about half their capacity, benefit from his work, the outdoors. He has left the mill to earn what he can cutting grass, shoveling snow, fixing roofs, attending to the gardens of more wealthy people in the more monied towns. Their English Gardener. He is sometimes introduced that way. *This is Percy, my English Gardener,* often followed by a giggle—he is, in some way, quaint to these people, with his clipped talk and his clipped hair and starched white trousers and shirt.

Martha works at the phone company now, in Information, the second shift. She took the work because the mill had become too much for Percy with its dank recesses and veils of dust. He works more hours now, out in the air, but the money is less and the seasons can conspire against him. So his wife also works, and makes no complaint, but after days outdoors he comes home and cooks for himself and sits reading, missing his wife.

In the evenings, after days in the sun, his fair skin is hot with the warmth of his burn. The muscles have the easy ache of a day working in fresh air, and it is late in the day especially that, alone, he must consciously think through the push and pull of inhalation and expiration. It's when he is tired that the breathing is most labored, most begrudging.

They have a dog now, a Corgi named Pierre. Pierre spends most nights curled on his small hooked rug, staring at Percy as he rustles through the newspaper. The dog's shallow pants are like an accompaniment to his own deep draws. The dog also seems wary of the newspaper itself, although Percy has never used a newspaper as discipline. When Percy finishes his reading and folds the newspaper over, the dog often scurries out of the room.

Most nights, Martha calls Percy at the beginning of her nine o'clock break, the ritual of the brief chat. But tonight it's ten o'clock and Percy can feel those low butterflies that come with a missed call, even though he knows she sometimes has to work through the break if someone has called out sick, or if it's an especially busy night—holidays and so forth.

"You want to . . . ?" he says to Pierre. The dog peeks around from the corner. It is likewise their habit that he takes Pierre for a walk as soon as he has hung up with Martha. Pierre is looking nervous. But Percy wants the phone call. He breathes more deeply, trying to settle himself. If he finishes his sentence, if he says the word, *walk*, Pierre will become so agitated that if the walk doesn't commence forthwith, the dog will urinate on the floor within moments.

"Ring," he says to the phone.

"Do you . . . ?" he says to Pierre, the dog's ears pricked at attention, his ears searching for the leash. Percy knows he shouldn't be teasing the dog like that.

The phone finally rings. Only a half-hour from the end of her shift.

"Hallo," Percy says, a hint of annoyance seeping into his voice.

"Percy?"

"Yes . . . who's this?"

"Percy, it's Eleanor. Well, something's happened. Martha's had a stroke, dear."

7. The fascinating glimpse into the life of a mature gentleman much unlike himself

After his morning walk on the palm-lined golf course, it is Percy's habit to return to his apartment, draw the shades, turn the air-conditioning unit on High Cool, and sit watching television, often with the sound off. Nothing on television interests him all that much. But other than the regimented segments of time in which he prepares meals, attends to his hygiene, or keeps his household in basic working order, it seems now, even as time grows ever smaller, that it is a fundamental struggle to simply bridge those hours. Nothing awaits him, particularly.

In the evening, when the sun drops and there is the notion of cooling in this tropical haze, Percy will loose himself from the four walls and go for another walk, in the dusk. The cocktail hour has arrived, and through many lighted windows he can see people, alone as he is, sitting in their chairs with tumblers in their hands, staring at the pale glow of the television. Another night falls on the lives of the people of Ocean Breeze.

But tonight, as he wanders back along the curb in the quarter-light, one of the apartments (the until-recently-vacant place four units down) has its door thrown open. From that door issues the music from a crackling Don Ho album. "Tiny Bubbles," unmistakably. He can hear, too, the low murmur of conversation.

Percy steps back onto the grass, cutting a wide arc so he

can see without being seen. He edges up to get an angle, and inside he can see a man about his age, wearing a Hawaiian shirt, white pants, and white shoes, all topped off by a white yacht cap with its life-preserver patch on the front. The man is behind a bamboo bar no more than four feet long. There are three stools in front of the bar, and on each stool is one of Percy's female neighbors, each sitting insouciantly with a martini in the hand and a cigarette in the mouth. The man seems to be carrying on a conversation with each of them at the same time, effortlessly. And, as it turns out, to be talking to him as well.

"Care to join us, bub?" the voice bellows from the apartment.

Percy steps to the doorway, feeling his shy smile creeping across his face.

"Thank you," Percy says, receding into the darkness. "But no."

For weeks after that, Percy avoids direct contact but can't help making sidewise arcing walks to his own unit that take him out onto the grass, in the settling darkness, with well-timed glances into the man's doorway. Always, three women occupy the three stools, and Percy is always amazed that it seems a rotation of many of the women from his complex—old ladies, frumpy grandmothers now transformed by the simple act of this man's arch hospitality. Percy avoids contact until one night when there is a commanding rap on his own door. When he opens it, it is none other than the man himself, standing in his doorway with two umbrella-adorned drinks in what appear to be coconut-shell cups.

"Hi, Percy!" he says.

Percy just gapes as the man forces one of the drinks into his hand.

"Call me Cap'n Irv, 'cause everybody does," he says. "The ladies told me your name. Let me tell you, you'd be wise to stop in to my little place some one of these nights. Ladies need some companionship and there aren't too many of us—men—around here. At least any worth a damn."

Percy nods. "You built a bar in your unit."

"I owned a tavern for thirty years. I guess behind a bar is where I'm most at ease. You can guess the name of the place— "Cap'n Irv's." That's what I've gone by all those years."

"Were you actually a captain?"

"In a different way. Not of a ship. I can't even swim! No. Back in the First War. Artillery. I can tell that you were there, too."

"Indeed."

"You were gassed."

"Yes."

"I hear you at night, when you're out walking. I know that cough"

"Yes."

"There are so damn few of us, left at this age, and all these damned women. I'm seventy-six. I don't feel half that."

Percy takes a sip from the drink. It's very sugary, and he has never been one for sweets.

"I'm just letting you know you're always welcome at Cap'n Irv's anytime. In fact, I could use a man like you."

Percy knows he won't go away until the drinks are done, so

he puts the coconut shell to his lips and sucks it all down. He
hands the empty cup to Cap'n Irv.

"Thank you," Percy says. "I most certainly will consider
that."

Afterward, in his apartment, Percy sits in his chair feeling
in his head the swirl of the drink, for he has never been much
of a drinker.

8. The eventful morning in which he is both delivered and condemned

Those who've gotten the worst of the gas are laid out in the
field hospital, nothing more than an open field set far from the
trenches. Percy is on his back. He rubs his eyes with the heels of
his palms, small relief, and tries hard just to keep breathing. All
around him he can hear the grasping of boys who, like himself,
have gotten it badly. The eyes burn beyond anything he could
have imagined, just as he had heard the officers describe the
effect in their briefings; he is enraged at himself for not having
put on his gas mask, even if there had been no order to do so. He
knows, from seeing other soldiers gassed, that right now there is
nothing anyone can do for him, even as his lungs shrink down
like slowly burning paper.

"Phosgene," he hears one of the officers saying. It is a new
and different kind of gas than the chlorine they had expected.
Nobody knows what happens after.

On the fourth day he is on his way back to England. He and
the others, eyes still covered by gauze wrapping, walk in a chain,
each man with his right hand on the right shoulder of the man

in front of him. They are loaded onto lorries to a temporary military hospital far from the front lines. Within a week of the battle, when the eye gauzes are removed and he tests his dim and squinting vision, he is put on a ship back across the Channel.

He is delivered to Oakwood Hospital, Rotherham, where he is surrounded by boys who have been wounded, many far worse— lost limbs, complete blindness, deep shrapnel wounds. He hears that virtually all the boys of Accrington, the Pals, are dead. Percy feels guilty in that there is not a scratch on him, only the deep burn under the ribs. Everyone is exceedingly cheerful, the ward clamorous with the laughter and badinage. In the newspapers there arc long columns of the dead, organized by regiment. His neighbors, the Walker brothers—Fred, Ernest, and Charles—have all died. Sixty thousand British men have died on that single day. Wesley is listed, the date of death actually two days after. Percy feels none of that euphoria of escape that resounds around him.

9. Some adjustments as they relate to the efficacy of one's own bodily capabilities

His wife looks at him always with a face of perpetual surprise, even after five years. The face he first saw at the hospital the night of her stroke, his uncertainty matched by her own mild but frozen-quizzical countenance, which has never changed. They're in Florida now, 1959, so much cheaper than the North, year-round grass to cut. Summers were difficult at first, but with the fans going all the time it became tolerable, the hot nights softened, the white-heated days somehow embracing. A little bungalow with burned-up grass and scraggly orange trees in the back.

They have no friends here, never tried. He has intuited in these years that she can't stand to be looked at, can't stand to be the person she now is, fettered inside the slack corporeal reality. Percy understands. They live in nearly complete quiet, even as the explosions in his head seem to have risen, coming back more often after the younger years in which he thought they were eradicated. He wakes up coughing, night after night. He wakes up from a drowning depth that frightens him, yet is always familiar, and not the only fear he truly feels in the spooling days of these late-middle years. He doesn't want to think of that creeping gas, that lunar battlefield. He doesn't want to think of his dwindling time. He doesn't want to think about Martha dying, but he likewise doesn't want to think about what will become of her if he is gone.

10. A decision ventured, without excessive or foolish delay

The convention of the event is that one accedes to the invitations that come one's way. Mrs. Gottlieb happens to be advancing such an invitation, and Percy allows himself to be swept into the swirl of the square dance. Staff takes turns calling the dance as the record plays behind. Mrs. Gottlieb smiles demurely. As he turns and pivots, his hand light and chary on hers, the opportunity is such that he can contemplate what would be so awful about a degree of relenting, some sort of acknowledgment that he just seems to be going on and on, and that some sort of plan does not invite the wrath of indeterminate gods.

"Percy, did you used to be a cowboy?" Mrs. Gottlieb says flirtatiously, and he can feel himself flush.

"Only tonight," Percy says, "Only tonight."

He can feel himself relaxing into something, a thought he rarely allows himself. That he might become friendly with a woman (these ladies, many of whom had no idea who he was, seem surprised and enthralled with his British accent: *Tillie, he tawks just like Cary Grant!*), and in that friendliness that he could begrudge himself some time in the world with some company, no matter how overdue he has become.

They dance on, changing partners, reconnecting, then veering off to the farther reaches of the Ocean Breeze clubhouse. Every so often, the needle skips on the square-dance record, and Eileen or Nancy from Staff interrupts their hand-clapping to push the tonearm forward, making everybody on the dance floor go into a momentary convulsive step to reposition their feet to match the beat. As it begins to feel as if the record will never end, Percy can feel the screaming need for his lungs to find more air. He is in a situation.

He can see Mrs. Gottlieb looking at him with a face turning toward horror. Ocean Breeze is not a stranger to various heart attacks, aneurysms, and simple weary passing, but not at a square dance—more often, people simply stay unmoving in their lawns chairs until someone notices they're still sitting out there in the dark. Keeling over at an Ocean Breeze social is, for the most part, simply not done.

Time has funneled down to that pointy notion, one in which he has to consider the idea that he is not going to make it through this dance, through the next lap of the second hand; but he wants to, wants so badly to complete this act and by doing so move toward the moment after that, in which something might be said, or ventured. The lungs feel as if they can seduce no oxygen at all. He wants, so much, to go on.

He cannot. He pushes off from Mrs. Gottlieb, whose face is instantly flushed and hurt, and he tries to maintain a controlled walk toward the fire exit. Pushing through, he is in open air, pulling hard into his lungs, his shrunken-leather lungs curled up under his ribs like dead leaves. He is alone in the dark, gasping in his pain, defeated once again, surviving once again.

11. *Particular memory that presents itself on a somewhat recurrent basis*

It starts at Rotherham, in that little recuperative bed, first as a flash of reconstitution. The first shards of the pieced memory, the most obvious things primary: the noise, the fear, the swimming struggle of body inside woolen uniform, of boots falling away under the vortical mud as it sucks around his puttees, the crush of his own gear holding him to the ground.

As the years go on, the dreams (Are memories really dreams, if they do not concoct things that have not happened?) seem to bleed of certain colors and retain in them the more structural elements: the swerving search for Wesley, never realized in the first breach of gas in its benign entry, not understood; the horizon of dead and dying, infinitely—yes, that, the faces and bodies in their dour uniformity, woolen forms bogged in their muck, cries of anguish, the sense in it all that the air has gone from the world.

And then, in old age, the reckoning. The burying of the dead, all of them, fields of them, the burying of the sense that this moment is ever resolvable—ever, possibly, somehow—by its nightly screening in his mind's recesses. Somewhere out here at the end of the line, they begin to recede, as if time has run out on all of them but him.

12. The outcome of situations that can only be planned to a certain extent

After Martha's funeral, he writes letters North to explain what has happened, and receives letters back that console and outrage him: *For the best; Not a surprise; Gone to a better place* . . . No one has come down but, on the other hand, no one was invited, none of these people grown so distant from him and Martha in the tightly circumvallated world. They cannot understand how he depended on her, even as he spooned food into her drooping mouth and carried her to the bathtub, her shrunken gossamer body. *You must be relieved . . . It must have been a burden . . .*

In the weeks after Martha has gone, Percy can only feel the sting of the fact, the moment: that their whole plan, the entire map of how it would be, has proven false. Him, standing over freshly turned soil, over the wife who would doubtlessly live on. Him, standing in the brilliant sunshine as his Martha settles into her darkness. Him, impossibly like this.

13. Some faint relief as provided by the carefully circumscribed art of the square dance

He hears someone coming out to get him. Staff tends to keep a wary eye, but what he hears is a man's harrumphing breaths, behind him. None other than Cap'n Irv.

"Bub . . . So you didn't die, then," Cap'n Irv says.

"Close, though," Percy whispers.

"Really? I was only joking."

"Oh."

"Well, don't worry, Mrs. Gottlieb will be okay."

"What happened to her?"

"You put her on the floor, Percy."

"Oh, good God."

"Staff checked her. She's fine. She landed softly. Those hips of hers."

"How horribly embarrassing, really though."

Cap'n Irv comes around to stand face-to-face with Percy, even though they are both in the dark.

"I didn't ever insult you, did I?"

"No, not at all."

"You should come by sometime," he says. "I'll mix you a drink. You can entertain the ladies."

"I've made a complete fool of myself."

"Maybe, but I doubt it. I think all in all, it went well. One small moment, is all. You've been in a war, what the hell's anything else?"

Percy thinks about this. "Can't really believe I got this far."

"You and me both."

They stand there nodding their whitened heads in the sultry darkness.

"Mrs. Gottlieb is owed restitution," Cap'n Irv says, and not without a lascivious air.

14. *The one moment of all that must always remain most considered*

He goes slower now, slower even than the slow swirl of a bunch of elderly square-dancing Floridians, slower than the record allows. A couple of dozen people, letting the music get ahead of them, no one mentioning that they are all simply waiting up for a man whose lungs betray him, always. Mrs. Gottlieb swings on his arm, smiling, unruffled by the past, the near past, or the rest of the past.

Strangers, all of them, a world of strangers that spread outside his door. But the touch of them is real, and they huff and wheeze as he does, and he somehow, miraculously, feels light on his feet, and carried along, on and on.

Street View

The original word, I might point out, was *Googol*. I remember that distinctly from my favorite childhood book. *The Answer Book*. By Mary Elting, and if not that, surely its sequel, *Answers and More Answers*. I Googled the book a while back to see which; sadly, both books seem lost to prehistory, defined here as prior to 1990. But the lack of the internet in my youth covers my tracks, even as it now works to haunt me.

The Answer Book was like a paper version of Google, if Google were limited to three hundred questions you didn't get to choose but were assured that "children asked most." *How is glass made? What happened to the dinosaurs? What makes a rocket go?*

When you finished that book there was a sense of completeness, but also the sense of all that was out there beyond one's view. What would the 301st question have been? In my rural childhood, when I closed that book, all that was left was the long expanses of sorghum that stretched out to the hot sky's edges.

"Googol" was the largest named numeral. A numeral one, followed by one hundred zeroes. Numbers like that seemed stupendous back then, but now barely make a dent. I feel a life in which, as I age, I have multiples of personas. The flow of information is overwhelming, and I found that the night I began to Google my possibly sad journey here. But circa 1970, *The Answer Book* was all I had, a meager meal in the end, staving off a ravenous appetite. The irony I find now is that for my own students, for whom facts and information lie boundlessly before them, they seem not to want to open the covers.

⌒

I grew up in Arkansas. The other night, I sat in my study in Cambridge and typed in the address of that first house, a faded bungalow shouldered onto Highway 65; on the screen of my laptop, rising like a fever dream from Google Street View, there it was. That shoebox of my misery. I could see them all, instantly: my mother, dropped ankles and rubbery skin, fretting on that low porch; my grandmother, wheezing in her housecoat; my father, shirtless, the billow of stink off his breath.

I worry that Street View might defeat my memory; I click the digital chevrons at the bottom of the screen, and the picture slides, and I am again gliding by that squat house, collapsing of its own humid cladding. I'm gliding as I did on that secondhand bike, spray-painted red, the underinflated tires thumping on the hot ribbon of Route 65—what my father called "The Road to Damascus," although the flow of northbound traffic indicated it was mostly "from." I don't remember sweating, but I must have, all the time, in that heat. I was ten.

⌒

Sometimes, then, I don't know how I got here. I rarely speak of who I once was, here in the rarified life. I am married to a woman who sits me down for a "serious talk" and says such things as, "I feel I need to be living a more textured existence." She cannot imagine the serious talks at that kitchen table in the house on Route 65, as poverty and alcoholism and despair closed in on my people. Then she looks at me looking at her, and accuses me of not understanding.

I wear all the right clothes now. The Oxford shirts and buttery loafers, the pressed chinos. After dinner I drink The Famous Grouse, on the rocks, from a crystal tumbler. I live in just the right place: I sit in my house on a leafy street, brick-sidewalked street (walking distance from the Yard), a street on which birds seemed to have been shipped in to sing their morning tunes.

So different than the machine-thrumming summer buzz of Arkansan grasshoppers. I had a drawl then; I speak now in the canned-soup vernacular of all the places I've been—not enough spice to make it interesting, not so little as to not be adequate to most.

My father would be ashamed of me.

But he died too early. Dropped dead in the rows in '72. On Google Street View, I find the next sad place, the apartment house in Little Rock where my mother and grandmother and I then lived on food stamps and church doles. Out there on Geyer Street, I discover, that house still stands, but barely: What was likely built to shelter a single family had then become diced into tiny compartments for unfortunates such as ourselves. Now, in my computer's image, that house stands beaten and boarded, the low chain-link fence collapsed and the scraggly trees in front as untrimmed as a drunk's beard.

But there, in the city, our fourth-hand television could get a signal, and the transformation began in small increments. In that small airless living room, I began to mimic those television voices, whispering those accentless sentences as holy mantras. I wanted to talk just like the Brady Bunch did. I wanted to talk like the Partridge Family. My mother would sit in her chair looking at me, saying nothing at all.

School was where I spoke that language loudly. My classmates would ask me where I was from. My teachers saw my hunger, and fed me; when, on my computer, I look at that boarded window to the right of the front door, I see beyond it my younger self, sprawled on the floor with pages, my limited facts and allotment of equations.

Could I have been my happiest then? Now, looking at my iPad in my dawn kitchen, with its Italian marble tiles and its massive culinary island, I look again at that boarded window on my MacBook and wonder. It was just myself, my mother and my grandmother. We endured those hot summers with only the rattling fan. My sweat coursed onto the books in that midday heat. My mother did find a way to get me the books, and I realize I never thanked her. At sunset, she went walking, alone, to get her air. She did so every night, night after night, coming home long after dark. One night she walked home early, with a man.

"This is Herbert," she said.

"No," is what I said.

Herb was a widower who had a house up on East Sixth Street. He was older, with two grown daughters; I think his only sin was loneliness, although I punished him for far worse, with my silence and derision. He spoke in that slow ramble, and when I had to speak to him, I responded in kind with my clipped new voices, my Transatlantic lilt. He was kind, although I'd have never admitted it then; it's harder for me to look at that house (which I never once referred to as "my house," always "Herb's house") on Street View, although even now it looks very well kept. The two cars parked on the lawn seem functional, the yard itself is green and trimmed and only burnt toward the curb. I suspect that some Herb progeny yet occupy that little place, which stands painted and clean among less-reputable neighbors. It could have been a haven. But I was already plotting my escape.

I didn't know what I wanted to do; I didn't know exactly who I wanted to be, but I sure knew who I didn't want to be. I explained as much in my college applications. It is the true remaining flaw on my permanent record of life (easily Googled now, to be sure, with various wiki entries, faculty profiles, and speaker bios) that I spring not from the Ivy League but from a less portentous place. But I recall the campus with happy memories. The day I got the letter and the pledge of scholarship at Bethany College, I knew this was the essential pivot of the plan. I can MapQuest the exact distance, door-to-door from Herb's to Bethany: 519 miles. A substantial journey, by any measure.

At Bethany, they were stout Lutherans (How many Saturdays I spent cheering on our football team, "The Terrible Swedes"?

I recall exactly our cheers from the grandstands: "Kor Igonem! Kor Igonem! Tjo! Tjo! Tjo!").

Regrettably, Google Street View has not much come to Lindsborg, Kansas. I refresh periodically in hopes of a more ground-level view, hope that camera-crowned Google car has finally breached its borders. But the blue line vaults straight up Kansas 4, through town, headed toward other places. Travelers had little to stop for. It is exactly in its plainness that I remember it.

Among those Nordic blond farm girls and soft-spoken boys, I continued to excel, overheated and driven. My letter of application had begun my shaping of my own story; happily, application essays are kept in locked places where my mother could never experience that betrayal. But I knew the way to a Lutheran's heart was to prostrate myself for salvation at their hands, and they were duly enthusiastic. Herb was recast as the heavy, my mother was substituted with someone sinful and irredeemable, and I was the boy in the wilderness. And they bought it! They even gave me clothes, so I wouldn't be embarrassed. Within days of arriving on campus, I began to again reshape the narrative all over again.

The unexpected advantage of attending a college called Bethany was that not only were there multiples (the teams of Bethany in West Virginia were also "The Swedes," although the Bethany in California fielded the "Bruins," more fearsome than even a Terrible Swede). But beyond that, the school's name, absent locus of eponymy, had the generic decentralized property of the accents I so astutely cultivated. A lot of people seem to think it's a good school located in Pennsylvania, or an up-and-comer in the Twin Cities. I disabuse no one of such notions. I arrived at history as my course of study, maybe owing to the endless facts of other times that one could drink in.

I never actually met a Terrible Swede in college, only very good-hearted ones. And the best of all was my professor of history, who was a gentleman farmer and amateur poet in the Edgar Lee Masters mode. He saw what I had, and he wrote the recommendations, and when I got the graduate fellowship, he bought me a celebratory coffee in that mostly dry town. I never bothered telling my mother where I was headed. At commencement, the president alluded to my salvation from hard times, to the confusion of my classmates, who'd been led to believe (notice me using the passive voice) that I was money from St. Louis.

I cannot view that old school from my stealthy Street View vantage, nor can I really see the faces of any of those peers, whom I scrubbed from my memory like the sheen of Kansas dirt that would blow in during spring planting. But the next place I seek on my computer represented a truer sense of arrival, thanks to that professor: When he'd coughingly mentioned he was himself a graduate of Dartmouth, it was frankly the first I'd heard of it. (I'd been led to believe the Ivy League consisted only of Harvard, Yale, and Princeton.)

Dartmouth, up there in the woods, is exceptionally well documented on Street View, even to the point of each crosshatched foot path on the College Green having its own blue line to drop onto. I can parachute my little Street View man, that similarly generic-and-golden avatar, onto exact spots. I can stand and again see places that still smolder in sky-clear memories.

I tend to linger especially on that curve of Cemetery Lane where, in a scene lighted only by a New Hampshire moon and its reflection off the deep February snow, I stood as Barbara walked off, disgusted at my intractability. I can drag and rotate the Street View image as if turning my head, canning those trees (still!) for her receding figure.

"I don't know who you are," she had said.

"I am who I am," I said. "Graduate student at Dartmouth. Eastern European history. Thesis proposal on the effects of Serbian exceptionalism."

She sighed. "So you are what you study," she said.

"In a way."

"Then I don't know who you *were*," she said, and to this I offered nothing. Not my accent, clothing, nor mannerisms betrayed a place of origin, or a story.

My own undergraduate students use Facebook addictively (even during my lectures!), pouring their minutiae out into the ether; I look at my own story and wonder if such transparency (more, really, than transparency, in its willful launch of facts into a universe presumed to care) could allow these children any chance for thrilling reinvention. My Barbara walked off into the shadows, and for the first time in my life I truly agonized, wondering if her love was worth disclosure. We never spoke again.

I realized, leaving Dartmouth with my first graduate degree, that I had acquired two firm addictions.

First, I knew I had become a collector of degrees. I chose not to pursue my doctorate at Dartmouth in order to add a different school to the list. I moved to New York, to Columbia, to begin my work in Early Modern Europe.

The second of my addictions was to change myself as I changed my location. As I left my graduate housing up in the woods, one of my female classmates said, "You need a haircut."

"No, I don't," I said, and firmly. The person I would be in New York wore his hair much differently.

Street View seems to have delivered a higher-resolution image of that apartment building on Morningside Avenue, and I tilt up into overcast sky to see the window of that walk-up on the fifth floor, with the fire escape outside, where as a man of long hair and fading history I smoked weed and romanced girls from Marymount. Histories indeed are like sediments; I accumulated personas in a way that, should I be asked something of what I had been, I had ready anecdotes and winning yarns. I look at that building on my computer screen and I smell the burn of the joint, and feel the throb of The Bird, and remember moist kisses but not the names of the girls being kissed.

Was I dishonest in all this? I would say not. I was who I was at any moment; my growing scholarly success suggested I was now who I should have been. In kind, I had escaped being the person I should never have been. I avoided judiciously any study of the South, with its Gothic tragedies, and I also abandoned in time the backwaters like Serbia, focusing instead on the great empires. Provincials are provincials, no matter where you go looking.

I was living on stipends and fellowships, a kind of welfare for the brainy, but New York fashioned my fashion. I roomed with a student named Will Featherly, of Short Hills, New Jersey; he became my primary observation subject. He was who he was. Never a doubt or veer. Money, smarts, and blond looks. Good at tennis. We shared a nodding and polite proximity; I was never invited by him to do anything or go anywhere. Yet I noted every nuance of his clothing. As I could squirrel money away, I accumulated like items, then never wore them. They were for the next stop. I could stare for hours at the custom-made shorts, with their mother-of-pearl buttons and hand-stitched plackets.

The doctorate came in quickly, and the offers of postgraduate fellowships were many, spread on the table as the array of people I could next be. I favored juxtaposition that year.

At UCLA, my faux-British accent returned to full flower, as did my bow-tie habit. It gave me a fish-out-of-water superiority that played surprisingly well in that sunny clime, both among my flip-flop-shod students but also my open-neck-shirteded faculty colleagues. I was presumed, with my Ivy degrees, to be a prince-in-waiting for higher stations.

Then I met Estelle.

The low hills west of campus, as it meanders toward Bel Air, come up on my screen vivid and bittersweet. Cars still triple-nose into the parking spaces under the canopies of apartment buildings on Midvale Avenue. Like pups pushing for the teat. The buildings are utilitarian, just grids of rectangular slider windows. I had my own "unit" of plain Sheetrock walls, a kitchenette, and a foam mattress on the floor, but I walked out that door each day as if to the manor born.

Estelle wore her South like a pair of chew-stained dungarees. She was a graduate assistant who came from Arkadelphia, "But I was born in Umpire!" she said in her bright twang, playing it up. Why she gravitated toward me I don't know, but I was to her like a familiar smell. I watched her from a distance in the fifth-floor lounge, trying to read her. But then I saw her likewise reading me, as through a two-way mirror that isn't fully silvered. Why me? She stared at me as if trying to place a face.

She was much younger, and by then no one I could have possibly known in my Arkansan youth, but she kept circling.

"Something about y'all that's hard to pinpoint," she finally said.

We began an affair of the most perverted kind: She took me to places like those I'd spent my life trying to escape, under the rubric of broadening my horizons. Cheap country bars with long-necked beers and thick-necked women, and Kuntry Kitchens tucked on side streets of far suburbs, with their steam pans of grits and hush puppies.

"How marvelous!" I cried from behind my bow tie, wielded like armor, as I sampled the fare of the hoi polloi. "Just this once, at least . . ."

She would stare me down. But I was partaking. We ended up in her frilly bed, making love under the ceiling fan, and, as

I withdrew, I had something like a fever dream. I saw below me the chilling alternative: This same girl, rougher and cigarette-smelling, on a soaked mattress in some cheap town; I saw us—she and the Me I might have been—sweatily heaving in an airless room. Grunting razorbacks come to root.

"What?" she said, alarmed at my expression.

"Nothing," I replied, knowing it was over.

"You're not who you seem," she finally said.

"Either are you," I said, a dagger to her: She was in fact a UCLA graduate student, not some hick with country sass. I know we felt more naked in that knowledge than we were in that moment.

⌣⌢

The problem is, I have no way of remembering her address, where via Street View I could skulk outside her window, with these complicated memories. She had driven me there in her pickup truck; after I left her place in rising dawn I simply walked away from the sunset. I want to say she was somewhere like Sunset and La Brea. I have walked my little golden Street View man up and down those sun-drenched streets (it occurs to me he must have been purposely modeled after Oscar), but we're searching for something we'll never find. All those places look the same, with only degrees of variation in a surprisingly depressing facade.

I went for a breakup beer with her a few nights later, in a country bar off Melrose. I patiently talked her through it and she laughed.

"Not unexpected," she said. "Because you know that I know."

"What do you know?" I said. I thought, *What am I afraid of? I've committed no crime.* Each degree on my wall was fairly earned, each publication the result of my own thinking and research. Why was she making me feel fraudulent?

But you get into it, maybe too deeply. She had rattled me.

"You know that, too," she said.

⌒

It was upon my return to school, this time to pull an accelerated doctorate in linguistics at Cornell (I was collecting Ivies on the premise that I'd otherwise risk backsliding, but here I had full teaching schedules and was treated as the peer I was). I was fully adult, nearly middle-aged, and I knew this would lock me into high stations. When I met Margaret, I knew she was the woman for me. The brittle patrician aloofness, the cultivated disinterest. She was a woman who exuded no secrets of her own, and no airs. But she came from the right kind of family in Utica, and craved larger venues. We married at her family church in a snowstorm, and I waited for the letter to come from Cambridge, which it did.

⌒

So here I sit in the middle of life, in my well-cut chinos and tailored blue oxford shirts and my glasses dangling on a cord around my neck, fumbling in the wine refrigerator for an evening's pleasure. Margaret tends to quiet nights as well, reading in the bedroom.

I stayed burrowed in my facts, my complex histories about which I published small monographs from the right presses, microscopic in their studies. I found myself an expert in the House of Habsburg, with special attention to the ancestry of King Charles II of Spain. The inbreeding of that family was stunning. They felt they had a superiority they cared not to share, and it ended up with infirmity, backwardness, and grotesque ugliness. Charles could not speak until he was four, nor walk until he was eight. The drive to preserve bloodlines had fouled them.

Early on, Margaret asked about me. I had built so many layers to my story I mostly started at Dartmouth and she was satisfied with that. I had no family anymore, I said, and at our small wedding there were the perfunctory academic colleagues, people with whom I kept a friendly distance.

In the early days of our marriage, the search engines were rudimentary sites such as AltaVista and Ask Jeeves, and to my horror, information about me began to trickle forth. The proper dynamic had always been for me to share who I was with those with whom I cared to share it. I didn't lie so much as deny the flow. Outside of my control, my life was being uploaded in small pieces. One night the phone rang, and I picked it up.

"Hello?" I said.

"Well, you sure did it," came that voice, the Arkadelphia twang flattened now like roadkill. "Got yourself all the way to Cambridge, just like the big plan called for."

"Estelle . . . Are you all right?" I asked. She sounded drunk.

"I'm fine," she said defensively. "Just *fine.*"

I asked her where she was calling from (these the pre–Caller ID days, when answering the phone had a not-always-pleasing air of mystery); she told me she was on a one-year visiting-prof gig, and then named the unfortunate Oklahoma backwater.

"And you're enjoying that, I hope?"

"Me? Sure. I'll take whatever jobs keep me going. I just looked you up on the internet and there you were."

Margaret called from upstairs, "Is that for me?"

"No, dear," I said.

"Married, too?" Estelle said. "That surprises."

"It's a normal thing to do."

"So why didn't we happen?" she said.

"Two people from different backgrounds," I said.

"I could tell it was more than that," she said.

"There was definitely some feeling," I said. "But that's moot now. My wife is upstairs."

"I get it," Estelle said. "Just askin', is all."

"No harm in that, I guess."

"Can I ask you the real question one more time?" she said.

"What would that be?"

"Where are you really from?"

I thought about this for a moment.

"I'm from my own imagination," I said, and listened to her sigh and quietly hang up.

⌐⌐

The nice thing about being accomplished and financially comfortable (but neither famous nor rich) is that you don't have to deal with people. You're freed from Walmart parking lots, from subways, from cheap bars. I remember that front door of the house on the edge of Little Rock, now boarded, and I hear the pounding of a landlord or collector of obligations; I'm aware still of my mother in the shadows, her finger over her lips: shh. I find peace in solitude, and in a kind of casual and unannounced reclusion.

My marriage had some passion at first. But Margaret saw my real thrill was in my many attainments. Things cool, always, even as my final destination, here at a great university, like-wise does. I walk to campus on cold mornings along the brick sidewalks of Kirkland Street, and then across the Yard to my office, passing John Harvard in his chair, the statue a study in rest and reflection. Home again at night, and to my computer after dinner, where increasingly I search out the old places, to arrive and look at them and see if they match my memory's eye. Historian, indeed.

Even County Road 20 has now been recorded, so that I can hover at its edge and peer over the low chain-link fence of Quattlebaum Cemetery, at the edge of the town of Bee Branch. My father is buried in that country graveyard. My mother is probably there, too, but I know not. I'd always thought I'd get the call, but never did. She may as likely be in Little Rock, at rest in the dry ground with the always-easy Herbert.

The Street View shot feels hot. The grass there is yellowed, and dry leaves dangle from branches. Drought. The buzz in my ear, I think, is the hum of those grasshoppers, praying in their own way. Grasshoppers thrive on drought, I recall, this bit of small retained knowledge. Not from *The Answer Book*, but from my doomed old man, standing in his overalls, afraid.

My father was a lonely person, I think. I wonder if any of him survives in me. I barely remember his face and assume I have, at this age, some remnant of it. He likely gets no visitors there in his roadside plot, other than my Street View ghost, peering from over the fence, unable to enter. All that survives of his short life of hard work is the chiseling of letters on his small marker. I, conversely, sit on a fall night in Cambridge thinking how I escaped that. I sit with my glass of expensive wine and my slices of aged artisanal cheese. On my trackpad, I now rotate the image away from the graveyard. What I see is the long winding retreat of Quattlebaum Road, stretching back into the deep rolling country. If I click those chevrons and I follow it, I do wonder how far it goes.

Writer Party

I 'm not really a writer; it's just that I write. I've done some
little books, and somewhere out there, a few distant critics
I've never met have spoken well of them. I've won a few awards,
even, the kind that at least make you feel you should keep trying.
But I'm not a writer, inasmuch as most people I know have only
the most vague sense of this. I work a job where books, and
especially made-up stories, find no purchase; indeed, I am just
the guy in the cube with the weird and semi-secret hobby. On
my tax returns, my occupation lists as "Clerical."

But on a soft September evening I am at, of all things, a
writer party. I've just had a new story accepted in a venerable
old literary magazine, and its fiction editor, a fusty, betweeded
man I've come to like immensely, has told me I need to get out
more. He's promised that if I come to his party, celebrating the
publication of work by one of the magazine's front-end writers,
that it will be good for me, and for my writing. Dutifully, then,
with my writing in tow like a socially awkward child who needs
to be mainstreamed more smoothly before all is lost, I show up
with equal measures dread and hope. I am a back-of-the-mag-
azine writer; in the cartoon version, I'm the one hanging off the
bus with one arm, my umbrella clutched in the other, my body

levitating with the forward thrust of the vehicle. I'm the last one on, but I'm on.

Here, in the Editor's living room, we all stand, drinks in hand. If you were at a higher vantage point of an adjacent building and saw us through the window of this Upper East Side apartment, you'd think of the Emperor Qin Shi Huang's Terracotta Army, all of us seemingly identical in earth tones and leather, wool and dandruff. All of us bathed in the amber of the Editor's galaxy of reading lamps. The women jangle in multicultural jewelry and their scents cloud and mingle; the men push their glasses up on their foreheads or run clawed hands through their longish hair. The variations, though, remain minuscule. As my father used to tauntingly say when I was a teenager experimenting with the Tears for Fears look, "I want to be different, just like everybody else!"

My partner, Stephen, is not with me; he's stayed home with the dogs. He's said, after once attending a book reading with me and witnessing its attendant patter, "If I want to be made to feel stupid, my high-school calculus teacher's number is right in the phone book." He's a lawyer, and I only lamely argue that they similarly have the arcane language and codes at their parties. "Oh my God," he says. "But I couldn't think of anything worse than a lawyer party."

So, on my own here, I stay in the corner and watch. And the Terracotta Army is not of one at all. Rather, to a more trained eye, it's like a forming universe with a swirl of gravitational pull creating floating bodies, waltzing planets, and moons. Near the host's bedroom, the poetesses, all gray-streaked and frizzy in their gravitas and their *authenticity*, are a coven of earth mothers, taking down (once again) Billy Collins. Billy Collins's success confounds them. "Billy Collins!" one shrieks, as one might shriek, "aerosol meatloaf!" They wear many bangles, the poetesses, and I suspect there's a complex system of signification there, not unlike those generals on the televised hearings with their kaleidoscopic ribbons. Power beads and ironic baubles and exotic hoops. They wear these as they do their obscure poetic forms, their villanelles and their pantoums and their rengas. They are like lawyers, urgent in their sidebars. I try not to oafishly admit my fear of any art in which you need an expert to explain to you why it's good. The light, then, I see is from the kitchen, and I move toward it.

"Jack!" the tangentially known novelist, Sandra Sellman, calls out to me. She's older, and stout, with that Marilynne Robinson doyenne air, sans Pulitzer.

"I'm Tom," I say.

She turns to her companion, a tall and squinting man.

"This is Jack," she says to him.

"Tom," I say, in a cough-like correction.

"Weren't you in Leslie Epstein's workshop, back in Boston? Isn't that how I know you?"

"No," I say. "I actually didn't go to graduate school. I think we met at a reading, years ago."

"I'm sure you had something to do with Leslie, but maybe that was another Jack. So have you published anything yet?"

"Well, three books so far," I say. "I have a story coming out in this magazine, which is why I'm . . ."

"Three books!" she says. "Good boy!"

I'm forty-four years old.

"Whose reading did I meet you at?" Sandra says.

"Ours," I say. "We did ours together. We had the same publisher."

"Oh, that's back when I was publishing with *David*," Sandra says. "I think David just, you know, *lost his touch*. So who do you publish with now?"

"David," I say.

I think of my Stephen, home with the dogs. Cavalier King Charles Spaniels. Buster and Killer. Furry tangles of love. They'll use your face as a personal salt lick; when you squeeze their necks, they are in utter rapture. They're easy, in other words. I know Stephen, right now, has them both on the furniture, even though it was Stephen's rule about the furniture. The dogs are rhapsodically watching Stephen watching some mindless movie. Cavaliers were bred for centuries to desperately crave love and attention. Me, I'm here among writers.

I'm not a heavy drinker, but tonight is an exception. I find a place on the far end of the couch with a bell-like glass of red wine.

"You're supposed to leave more room in that glass," someone says of my brim-filled vessel. "All that room is supposed to be for the *nose*."

At the other end of the couch, a man in a black turtleneck and with hair like a forsythia bush is going on about those big lecture-hall classes.

"Some of them are four or five hundred students," he says.

WRITER PARTY / 61

"I always hated those kinds of classes," I say, trying to not just be sitting there alone at the end of the couch.

Everyone in the conversation looks at me. *Blink blink.*

"No," the man says. "You're so completely wrong."

"It's just an opinion," I say.

"Based on what?"

"Based on having been in those classes," I say.

"You must not have been a very good student, then."

I shrug. "It was a really long time ago."

"It's up to the student to understand how to appreciate it."

"I always thought it was for the university to save money."

The man snorts. "Well, well, not quite."

"I'm so sorry," I say. "I should never have butted in on your conversation."

"Oh, no, not at all," he says, homing in on me like a student caught sleeping in the front row. "It's always good to disabuse the misinformed."

"So you teach big classes," I say.

"Certainly."

"And you enjoy them."

He looks at the others, like, *Do you believe this guy?*

"It's not at all whether I enjoy them," he says.

"I see . . ." I say. "I guess it's just that in those big classes, you don't get to really, you know, converse with the professor."

His face says, *Aerosol Meatloaf.*

"But that was never the point, for me to have to talk with *children*," he says. "It's that the students have the privilege of hearing me in Socratic dialog with myself. They can hear the flow of my ideas without the insipid questions."

"What do you teach?"

"Motifs of Narrative Theory in Greek Mythology."

"That's the name of the course?"

"The name of the course is 'Intro to Reading.' But what I teach is motifs of narrative theory in Greek mythology."

The silence hangs, even in this room of chatter. The man to my right sticks his hand at me. "My name is Walt," he says. "I produced the first staging of 'Rent' ever to be done in Papua New Guinea . . ."

I begin then to clear out room for nose in my bottomless glass, which reverbs like a tuning fork when it clicks my teeth. I need to go for a refill, as quickly as I can.

The Columbia crew has entered the fray. They all, young men and women, wear the heavy-framed black glasses, as if Columbia hands them out at graduation, rolled up in the diplomas. They're genial, quiet, and a bit overserious; they are a riot of plaid, and of boots, outfitted for the wilds above Ninety-sixth Street. Tattoos and lyricism. Lumberjacking their prose with soft hands, undoubtedly. I seem swallowed by them, like a square old Dad tagging along, their gauntlet mixing with the ragged line for more drinks. Someone bumps me and my empty wine glass dings in a plaintive moan. There's much talk of "Knopf" around me, the word issued from reverent and acolytic lips, a benediction with a hint of the unintended sneeze. *Ki-nopfff. . .*

"Did you know that Stephen King has a book on *how to write*?" one of them says, clearly incredulous. Stephen King

seems the aerosol meatloaf of MFA programs everywhere, and
even here you can see clots of people forming based on their
grad-school affiliation, like street gangs in their colors. Over
there comes the Irvine crew, in their "don't-you-even-fucking-
know-about-Irvine?" smirks, and here is the Virginia group, with
their J. Press insouciance. A group of clustered and nonaffili-
ated mock-Mary-Gaitskills, all platinum hair and wary, stunned
looks, pass silent judgment on us all. When an Iowa Writers'
Workshop grad walks by, searching for the Jim Beam, one of
the Gaitskills says in a flat sotto voce, "Iowa, and no book yet."

I've told Stephen I might be out on the late side, but the clock
is spinning backward now, as in a black-and-white time-travel
movie. But I'm afraid I'll overshoot my era, and land right back
at the beginning of this party.

"My agent says no one will be able to resist," a passerby says.
Then I see Kerry, entering.

I can barely remember how I even met Kerry, but am always
happy she remembers me. What a writer she is, and she's duly
rewarded now with her Ivy League appointment and line of fine
books. She's in the Norton Anthology, her stories skimmed in
the wee hours by freshmen everywhere.

"Tom," she says. "The hermit himself!"

I shake her hand. "Not a hermit, except from this world."

"I saw you had a new book," she says. "Congratulations."

"I really appreciate that." She is a bit older than me, but
there was some point in the past when she had shown herself
to be an encouraging, decent person. She seems abnormally
normal, for a writer. I only started writing very late in life, after

years of telling myself it was a really stupid idea; the fact I was introduced to her early on has made the literary thing at least a shred more comfortable.

"How are the dogs?" Kerry says.

I love that she remembers the dogs. She has an odd way of coming upon me in the park with them, those times when I tell the dogs it's Silly Time, as if dogs need to be told that. She busts me constantly, and it apparently has endeared me to her. The dogs are always a happy conversation. I say, "They're —"

"Kerry, my darling!" comes an exclamation from back and to the left.

It's Sandra Sellman, in full intercept mode. Sandra walks right into the middle of my sentence, and just pulls Kerry off somewhere. Kerry looks over her shoulder at me, mouthing *Sorry!*

Intercepts all around, the pinging of writers trying to up their status by entering other writers' personal space. If I made a Euler diagram of the dozens of people in this vast apartment, with the outer circle being all those people who are writers, and the inner circle being writers whose books were bought and/or read by anyone else at the party, it might look like a pizza with a singular pepperoni. Kerry is read, for sure. She is the truly famous writer in the room, also. The writer who is the subject of the party is known, but possibly not even read.

Who reads any of us, really? In my case, the answer is "not many," that's for sure, but at least somebody bought the books. But I worry when I can't sleep that those were all library sales, based on certain positive reviews, and that all over the land my books are shelved but sadly uncracked, virginal.

"That damned cover design killed my sales," another voice near me says.

Who reads us? Really?

If I made a Venn diagram of two circles, one being readers of books on subways, and the other being books published by the people at this party, it actually couldn't be a Venn diagram, because to have a Venn diagram the circles have to actually touch.

"Clive Cussler!" a poetess shrieks from across the room, the others bending over as if collapsing.

"Mary Higgins Clark!" says another, and I must admit that is a funny name.

I see across the room that someone, of the well-known form called the "MFA type," is driving between Kerry and Sandra, a wedge into the wedge. I can't tell for sure, but she may be carrying a full manuscript in her generous clothing.

"Who are you again?" a woman says to me.

"I'm Tom," I say.

"What did you write?" she says.

I tell her the name of my last book.

"Well, I don't know it," she says, turning.

I see a writer whose book I just read, and liked. She looks somehow fuller, or possibly flusher, than on her author photo. Then I realize the photo has been desaturated to digitally fade her to-be-expected wrinkles. She must be in her early sixties; her photo is like the geisha version of her frank, spored face. But yet I give her credit; when I see some of these writers, I think their jacket photos must be of their children, who look so much like them. We all want to remember those days. This author, I think, will continue to desaturate herself until, in her late-life books, she is a ghostly apparition, floating translucently over her own words.

"Isn't she a bitch?" a guy next to me says.

"Excuse me?"

"I see you can't stop staring at her."

"She's just become so *desaturated*."

"That's being kind."

"You don't like her?"

"Don't like her? After what she did to my book in *The Times*?" I gape.

"You must remember what she did to me in *The Times*."

"Uhh . . ."

He stares at me.

"You don't even know who I am, do you?"

I shrug.

"So then you must have come to the party *with* a writer, did you?"

I'm standing at the bar, filling my glass again. The rented bartender is watching me now, unamused. Tonight I will definitely spring for that cab in lieu of staggering home up Eighth Avenue. I'll be hurtling forth, with the windows open to the wind, to rejoin the only people who really matter—my man and my dogs.

Two guys behind me are speaking in hushed but unmistakably intense tones.

"Older editors are conditioned to Courier 10, whether they realize it or not," one of them says. "They've spent their lives reading manuscripts in Courier 10, and if you throw them Times New Roman 12, it's as if they can't even *process* it."

"But I use Times Roman 12," the other one says. "Is that why I'm not getting published?"

"I said fuck them all, and I just went with Cambria," the first one says.

The Editor has plenty of bookshelves, all enjambed with handsome volumes. Most people I know who even have bookshelves fill them now with family photos, mementos, and out-facing dishes, so it's good to even see bookshelves used for their eponymous purpose. Indeed, as well, there are piles of sideways books stacked on the floor in front of the shelves, piles two and three feet high. Now, one partygoer, a young man looking unsteady, sits atop a pile of the wider books, putting his head between his knees. A girl stands next to him, saying, "Breathe."

"Is he all right?" I say.

"His editor just dumped him," she says. "It was a setup, to do it here in a public place so he wouldn't make a scene."

"That's awful," I say. "He kind of is making a scene."

"He'll live," she says. "Mine dumped me with a text message."

Kerry has been intercepted again, across the room. I wonder why she even comes to these things. I wonder if when she was a little girl, writing unicorn stories with a thick pencil, she thought, *Someday I'll be endlessly intercepted at writer parties*. It's like the Telephone Game, as she gets wrenched from one person to the next. But here she is, and here am I.

Lunch? she mouths to me across the room.

Silly Time, I mouth back.

The tweedy Editor wanders up to me as I put on my coat.

"So soon?" he says, helping me on with it. "We didn't even have a chance to chat."

"I know you have a million people coming at you," I say.

"You'll come by the office, then," he says.

"Of course." I shake his hand.

"Soon," he says.

"Undoubtedly."

"We'll talk about your overuse of indefinites in your story," he says. " 'It is' a problem," he says merrily, using quotation fingers to drive home the point.

I nod.

"Not your scene here, then?" he says. He seems worried that it's not.

"It's just me," I say. "I've never really socialized with writers. I think I'm a bit off the map with all that."

He pats me on the back. "Yes, indeed. Writers can be difficult, and loud, and needy."

I nod.

"But just remember," he says, with unmistakable portent, "someday you may desperately need a blurb from one of these people . . ."

When I get home, Stephen is asleep, on his side, fully clothed. The dogs lay against him, Buster at the small of his back and

Killer at his crotch, as if they have dragged him down from the avalanche and are virtually willing him back to life with their body heat—even as, in point of fact, they are draining him of his own. Their eyes bulge at me, and their tongues hang, but they stay at their stations. I toss the throw over Stephen's legs, pat his hip, and I go to the little office we have, where my desk overlooks the airshaft.

I know I should sleep. The blue-green screensaver lights the room in an aqueous glow, as if I'm treading on the ocean floor. I wearily unsnap my wristwatch, and as I put it down, I bump the desk enough that the mouse moves, the screensaver terminates, and the room goes weak white. I face the screen, then, blinding with my digital paper and my digital Times Roman 12. There's my new story, halfway done, the one I know I've been thinking about all night.

I sit and read the last sentence. *I'm too old for this shit,* I think. As with drinking, I've found that I start at this earlier in the day, and I stay at it later at night. I've let it affect my job, my relationship, my finances. My life. I can't stop, though, as if it were even voluntary to do so. So, late at night in a quiet room, I type out another sentence of another story. It feels good, so then I go ahead and type another. I should sleep now, but I won't for a while. The whole time, I keep trying to convince myself I'm not actually a writer.

David

V ideo games straight through that night, the digital binge, though this has long ago stopped being playtime to him. The headphones clamped on his ears; the thunder of his battle blasting through his brain. Beyond the earcups the noise issues as an insistent static filling the dark, enough for his mother to hear through the thin wall to her room. Awakened by that muffled version, she comes pushing in. He looks up at her thick shadow filling the doorway and sees her head shaking and motioning to listen to her. He drops the volume and slips one side of his headphones away from his ringing ear.

"What?"

"David, it's past three in the morning," she says in that hoarse whisper.

"Yeah, I have a big test tomorrow," David says.

"Why do I not believe that?"

"Can I just do this then?"

The door shuts, the whoosh of her exasperation tailing it. He reconjures his thunder and plays on, too enervated to sleep anyway. He wants to find his way to a seamless crossing of a threshold.

No one is a stranger here, not any of the endless enemy com-
batants that come at him in waves. He knows them and lives with
them. Every enemy in *Grand Theft Auto* has traits of those who
are actually his enemy. Every monster on *Fortnite* has its des-
ignated analog in real life. Many a night he's lain awake in bed,
forging those links. There's a Wei Cheng in every homeroom;
there's a Stretch Joseph around every turn in the long corridors
of Memorial High School. In these games, he fires not at shadowy and encoded figures but at every catalogued humiliation
he's been subjected to, every long-held memory. It's the better
moments that seem harder to remember.

His night world is far better than his day world. In the night
world, he hides in the eclipse and controls all moves. In the day
world he feels as if walking, always, through fire and glass. In the
night world he feels the power and pleasure of erasing his tor-
menters, without mercy. In the day world he is the tormented, in
endless cycles, like a computer restarting to renew the struggle.

He knows he's different. He's reminded of that endlessly
throughout each day. Shoved because he hates to be touched.
Laughed at because he never laughs himself. Made the target,
the butt, the easy punchline. Everybody is embedded in their
assigned roles, just as in the video games; he wonders how hard
those boys on the football team analyze why they do what they
do, or if like the hordes on his monitor they are simply pro-
grammed to be that way. He has dreams sometimes that everybody but himself is a robot; he alone has the capacity for emo-
tions and pain. Around him, no one gives away the truth of this.
People, he finds, are mostly one-dimensional.

But the plan. Set now. A progression that has gone from vengeful daydreams, to the first tentative Googlings, to the night he began to realize he was thinking of all this as very real, and unavoidable. There was a power to that. Every morning thereafter he has stepped through those double doors at the high school, making tallies of those most worthy of the fire and glass he will hold tightly in his own hand.

And he'd thought eighth grade was as bad as life could get. After that coming of age among the same twenty-one kids of his neighborhood elementary school grade, and yet feeling more adrift with each ensuing year, he'd ended up in a high school that was like a vast netherworld. Memorial was a dystopian big-box complex, ruled by hordes of hoodied boys far less willing to accommodate him the way he had been. Shoves and shoulders throughout freshman year; him going glaze-eyed and slack. Sophomore year became more than physical. He was the outlier, and always had been; he walked the halls staring at the floor while they escalated the taunts and pushed him a little harder. Was he a retard, a freak, a fartknocker? Did he commit sexual acts on various animals? Had he been aborted? He didn't know what they wanted from him, or how to change. Being different from them was the only way he knew how to exist.

The most enthusiastic of his antagonists was Colin, the relentless instigator. A lacrosse player with much self-regard, Colin one day began the practice of walking behind him in the hallways and flicking David's ears with a snap of his fingers.

Colin, daring him to turn. The ear, stinging; the wave of derision behind him burning as he trudged on. All he wanted was not to be noticed at all; David's longstanding and comfortable invisibility was now largely negated by Colin's seemingly inexhaustible need to expose him.

Then, the one day. Going to homeroom, his stomach the usual knot, waiting for whatever was gaining on him. Then the sting of the ear, the laughter; then him turning, for the first time, wheeling around to face Colin, who stood a head taller and seemed both surprised and utterly amused at being confronted. Others, in the corridor, paused to watch.

"I want you to stop now," David said, aware of the shake in his voice.

"Oh, you do?" Colin said, as if this had been a mutually agreed-upon morning ritual.

"Yes, I do."

"But then how do we stay friends?" Colin said.

And then the roar of laughter around him. David turned and instantly came another hard flick on his ear, more aggressive and geometrically more painful.

Such is a moment that isn't forgotten when one concludes there are few solutions. This was that moment. David watched Colin strutting away, and wondered if a boy like this truly understood what he'd just effected.

⌒

David and his mother had lived in this apartment building for three years, since his father took off. The paternal exit was before dawn and lacking explanation, at least to David. Maybe a new girlfriend; maybe just sick of who he was. David had always known he was an embarrassment to his father; he felt the shame every day of the rolled eyes, the shaking head, the stretches of shut-down silence. But likewise, David could recall no time in which he'd ever been really shown how to do things any differently, as if he had no real talent for change.

The Exit had led to a time of austerity. His mother periodically wept at the kitchen table as she sorted out the bills. Mostly she stayed in bed in her room, watching the political channels, an unbroken screech of people shouting each other down and railing against their enemies. She worked the second shift as a medical secretary. On weeknights, that left him to make his own dinner, often just gorging cookies, and to do his homework (at least in theory). He was bored by most of his enforced education, but he retained what was said in class and that proved enough to pass his tests. He was more lately flirting with the idea of dropping out. Most afternoons he sat at the kitchen table eating microwave pizza and looking out the window, waiting for the Lindbergh Baby.

The baby was the child of a couple in the house over the fence. He didn't know their names; in his history class, a girl had done a PowerPoint on the Lindbergh case and he'd been nearly jolted by how much these two babies looked alike. The mother looked nothing like Anne Lindbergh, and the father was much too hipsterish and earthbound to suggest any analog to Charles. They were young and clearly in the thrall of parenthood. David would stay at the window frame, in the shadows, taking it all in. And every time now that he sat at his window waiting for that glimpse of the mother and her baby, he was retched by the thought of its delicacy, its vulnerability to what was proving a very brutal world. He wondered if he had ever been doted upon the way the Lindbergh Baby was, and whether his parents lost the interest as he grew into the awkward, ill-fitting boy he knew he was but had never once intended to be.

⌒○

David had long since arrived at the presumption that high school was a netherworld as evil as those in his games, but with less control over outcomes. There was a reason no one in video games "talked it out," as the new counselor had once suggested David do after he was knocked down by a football player in the parking lot and left crying on the ground with skinned knees through his tattered pants. He'd been brought to this counselor by a teacher who appeared mostly to be "taking action" only because David lay weeping on the ground between her and her car door as she was heading home.

The counselor was a man in his thirties who looked as if he might have been a football player once himself. Mr. Deekins.

"Are you sure it wasn't just an accident?" Deekins asked. "Accidents happen sometimes, don't they?"

"Well, he didn't even apologize. He just kept walking."

"Maybe he thought you were at fault. Maybe if you talked it out you would find a resolution."

David stared at this man. "Like I said, he walked away."

"Maybe you should work harder at getting along with people. Do you even have any friends?"

"People avoid me now. People who might have been my friends won't go near me, because they don't want to get treated like I do."

"Well, that just sounds like an easy excuse," Mr. Deekins said.

⌒

In the night world, there was no mercy, and no presumption of one. David's condition was probably a contributor to his mastery of these battles. In *Call of Duty,* his time-to-kill value is 99th percentile, just like his math PSAT's; the end of this particular spectrum was kind to him. He steadily leveled up, effortlessly, from PFC to Prestige. In one manic stretch, he'd Prestiged in sixteen hours and eleven minutes; when it was done he'd gorged on ice cream, masturbated, and slept thirteen hours. When he entered a group game he was feared, and that felt better than anything: the falling enemies, the body counts, and the melodic rattle of an AK-47. Which made it all the more untenable that he should walk into school each morning to withstand the assaults of gawky lacrosse players.

⌒

For a time, David felt as if his US history teacher, Mrs. Leone, was on his side. She was young and relatively new at the school. She seemed a very happy person. She didn't exactly act friendly to him; she certainly didn't advocate for him. But what she did do was softly put the brakes on Colin and a few of the others in a way that nearly felt as if she were defending David, silently. In class, Colin would edge toward crossing one line or another—talking, throwing things, texting, and sitting as he did—gathering himself to find yet another way of setting upon David. For this reason, David hated to be called on, as he was on a particular morning of a particular week. The question had to do with the Treaty of Versailles.

"Who was responsible?" Mrs. Leone asked him.

"I don't understand the question."

In the back, he could hear Colin grunting to his friends: *He's so fucking stupid.*

Mrs. Leone made a sour look, and he wasn't sure if it was because of him or Colin. "What don't you understand about my question, David?"

"If you're asking who was responsible for creating the treaty—which were the allies, or who was forced to take responsibility for the war because of their aggression, which was Germany."

He's such a fucking show-off.

Mrs. Leone nodded. "I guess I could have framed the question better. I was asking you the second part."

"Germany was forced to admit responsibility, although the German people saw themselves as having had to do what they did. The resentment they felt pretty much led to World War II."

"True, but you're getting a little ahead of yourself. But a good answer."

"I'm very interested in aspects of war," David said, to silence behind him, then a held-in snort.

The bell rang, and he entered the transitional hell of the corridor, where danger was at its highest. He got a shove from behind, but it felt almost half-hearted.

"Don't bother trying to show off to her, because she's already taken," Colin said.

"I'm well aware she's a married woman."

Colin and his boys broke out laughing. It seemed anything out of David's mouth was worthy of ridicule. "Yeah, you'll need to wait your turn," he said, flicking David's ear with renewed vigor.

⌒

When the package arrived on his doorstep, in a most highly illegal fashion, his mother simply pushed it at him without a shred of curiosity. He'd gone online, had crossed over to the dark web, and found the calculations to this particular connection—resulting in this delivery of a semi-automatic, short-barrel Oracle—more interesting than any math problem in Mr. Babcock's math class; it was amazing what illegalities could be committed via the internet if one had enough money and had cracked the particular codes meant to skirt governmental surveillance. The gun was clearly stolen, and priced down out of desperation to unload it; the buy was easy—he'd been lifting loose money from his mother's handbag for years. This particular stash was to have gone to a new PlayStation 4 Pro.

His mother was coming in from work when she found the package leaned against the storm door, and she showed no curiosity. She just wanted her shower and her drink. The return address might have suggested certain intrigues, with its inscrutable blankness. He felt the relief of slipping this by her, a deadly instrument buried in swaddles of foam and bubble wrap. But he had almost hoped she'd ask, just so he could push back at her. What had she ever done to lighten his pain?

She disappeared into her bedroom and the TV went on. He went to his own room and used a steak knife to open the box. He spent some time just looking at his weapon laying on his desk top. He couldn't have said he wanted to do anything with it. This was the secret power, just having it. He'd just leveled up. This was the power, knowing he held something over anyone who chose to cross him. And secret powers were always to be held in reserve. Secret powers remained secret.

But then the next morning in class, he wondered if some-thing had given him away. Mrs. Leone seemed to take some note of him in a way not taken previously.

"What is it, David?"

Everyone turned to look at him.

He had always been invisible to all. He had no idea what he'd done to elicit this question, neither smiling nor smirking, neither angry or upset. Just sitting there.

"Nothing, Mrs. Leone."

"Okay. But let's talk after class."

"Am I in trouble?"

"Not that I'm aware of."

He could feel Colin's glare scorching the back of his neck. He absorbed nothing of the remaining class as the seconds ticked to the bell. As all others leave, he stayed in his seat.

"I'm sorry, you just seemed . . . different . . . today," Mrs. Leone said.

David shrugged.

"Is everything okay?"

"Everything's fine."

"Is there something you want to tell me? Something on your mind?"

He could see her affect, her low-grade irritation with his presumed withholding.

"Then you should get to your next class," she said.

In the nearly empty hallway, he hurried to algebra, a different man. He had been noticed in a way that could only be for one reason.

That night, he found himself on a porno website instead of playing the usual games. Something stirred up by the slightest of attentions, he knew. But Mrs. Leone's sudden attention had to have been noticed by the girls who surrounded him but had never seemed to see him. They were resolute in their non-acknowledgment, until maybe now.

The next morning in school, it nearly felt as if he was just someone else, someone who could just go along. But Colin and his friends had taken notice of him being noticed.

"Here he comes," Colin said. "Hey, Player, you think you're special?"

"Everyone is special in their own way," David said.

Colin gave a sidelong glance to his friend Levi, the football player, who said, "That's why everybody fucking hates you."

"Why? Because I'm special?"

"Because you talk like a fucking freak."

"Maybe you listen like one."

He was hit faster than he realized the blow was even coming. Levi hit him open-handed, but incredibly hard, and on the ear. David felt as if he might fall, but he got control of his buckling legs and stayed on his feet. The two of them were already down the hallway, laughing; no one else in the swirl was even looking at him.

Another border crossed, and he had no idea why. He had the swelling urge to cry but did not. Again, Mrs. Leone zeroing in on him, but this time he avoided any eye contact, and she said nothing.

His ear still rang hours later. As he left school, he kept his head down, seeking nothing more than an escape. But someone was on him, a sidewalk shadow next to his own. He looked up and was surprised. Billy Devin. Billy who had acted like a stranger since the end of freshman year.

"You know what's going on, right?" Billy said.

"What are you talking about?"

"So you're like the only one who doesn't know."

"I don't need you coming at me, too."

"I'm trying to help you out."

"So what don't I know?"

Billy looked around and then dropped his voice.

"I've only *heard* this—"

"Heard what?"

"So that kid Levi, who hit you? He's been having sex with Mrs. Leone in his truck for about a month now."

His ear had developed a persistent ring on the way home, like an alarm that couldn't be turned off. He put his finger in his ear and twisted it, as if there was a switch to deactivate, but which he could not. Walking, he didn't feel angry at Mrs. Leone. She was a victim of Levi, too, he thought. She was confused, clearly. She was set upon by the same hordes who beleaguered him.

He wasn't going to do any homework. He was now ready to drop out of school, immediately. He could fool his mother for a while. She slept late; if he cleared out at eleven in the morning, he could reenter the apartment by four, after she'd gone to work.

He was unburdened by his decision. What came next was of no concern to him. He'd eat and sleep and disappear into his games. Happiness was close by now. As he came down the walk pulling the keys out of his pocket, he heard someone shouting. He turned and saw Lindbergh Mom, sans Lindbergh Baby, coming up at him. She had her phone up, filming.

"Yeah, you!" she said. "So why are you always spying on me?"

"I, uh . . ."

"Are you some kind of freak?" she asked. "Are you a stalker or something?"

"How can I be stalking someone when I'm sitting safely in my own room?"

"Don't be an asshole," she said. "Because I really don't like assholes."

"I was just looking out my window."

"Every time I look up, I see you staring at me."

"It's really not about you," David said. "It's your baby."

She was looking at him through her phone, and the phone hid her face from him. He turned away from the lens.

"Okay, you want me to call the police now?" she was saying.

He had his house key near the lock, but his hands were shaking.

"Don't walk away from me," she said. "Should I call the police, or what? Talking about my baby like that. What do you have to say?"

He turned back to her.

"I'd say you should call the police. I *admire* someone who's looking out for a child. I *respect* someone who is going to do that. I don't know what the police would say about someone looking out his own bedroom window, but I'm sure we'd all figure it out. But protecting your baby is worth it. So yelling at me for no reason is better than not yelling."

"I'm watching you now," Lindbergh Mom said, lowering the phone, as David fumbled with his key in the lock. "So don't even think about whatever it is you're thinking about."

⌒つ

The police didn't come. He played the games into dawn as he so often had. He heard his mother coming in from work, but she didn't knock on his door. Tonight was always going to be sleepless, he realized; he played with a visceral anger that found release, hour after dark hour. Whatever relief he'd had earlier about not going back to school was muted by a rising anger that he'd been defeated. He thought of his hidden gun. Its secret power had been sadly short-lived. He had meanwhile accumulated a deep cache of reasons to act. His mind held facts extremely well, sometimes too well: That he had catalogued every indignity, every attack on him, and every humiliation probably made him far angrier than if he were a less-intelligent person.

He had known a particular day was coming, but not the exact day. He gleaned nothing special in the way of anniversaries or milestones; another day that was another day. But tonight, he decided that day would come very shortly.

Through the double doors, his vision narrows. He has the light-headed and merry and edgy feeling of great adventure plopped like a topping upon a crust of resentment and fury. He guesses he must already have been spotted on the security camera; he hasn't been in school in a month and now here he is, lugging an oversized backpack. He quickens his step, trying to get to that place he knows the enemy gathers. He is in his own game now, a character controlled by something bigger.

Out into the hallway, feeling weightless, as if a holographic version of himself, slow-walking to his destiny.

II. THE AFTER

The media, of course, had gotten it all wrong. He read accounts of himself that bore no resemblance to reality. Up popped Lindbergh Mom on the television news, saying "He creeped me out. I felt I was in danger." One and another kid from Memorial, most of whom he'd never laid eyes on in his life: "Everybody was scared." "I wasn't surprised."

Mrs. Leone, saying, "He pushed away anybody who tried to help him."

He, the victimizer? He, a *monster*? He had moved in a world that no one understood. He had chosen to answer threats everyone now dismissed. The booking photo of him was of another person: wide-eyed, weak, pale. He looked as if he might have been crying, though David had no memory of that. In fact, he felt as if he was looking at another person altogether.

H is mother avoided the television cameras in those first days, holding a hand over her face as she ran from her car to the front door. She said nothing; he heard nothing from her. A month into it, he wrote her a letter. It came back with no forwarding address. By the time of the trial, he had no expectations he would hear from her again.

On the cellblock, the faces looked the same as they did at the high school. That loathing. That dismissal. Prison at least was favorable in that they kept people separated from one another. David was mostly alone, as he had always been.

But the difference was in the lack of indifference. He saw the flashes of real hatred. He saw the vengeful impulses just below the surface. He was protected by guards who loathed him just as completely. Even when the cell doors opened, he was more inclined to stay away from the others. Like high school, like his games, like the world, human nature skewed toward power and domination.

Solitary rooms, solitary days, solitary meals. No different, really, from anything else.

They didn't allow video games at this level of security, though constant rumors circulated that they would be, soon. He tried to conjure in his mind the greatest victories in the games he'd played night after night for so long, but they failed to form in a way that he found satisfying. He had no happy memories other than those.

He was by far the youngest. He'd been tried as an adult and as an adult he would serve his time. The cellblock TV went on endlessly in the common room, and he found little appeal in the political shows the self-styled "cerebral" inmates watched, or the sports the rest of them flocked around. There was a bank of old IBM computers inmates could use, but no internet. He borrowed old CDs from the prison library that held voluminous tests on criminal law. David tended to sit at the edges of each group, absorbing little but somehow going catatonic from the noise and light. *I'm really not even supposed to be here.* He checked the law CDs out of the library, searching resolutely for the loophole that he couldn't even yet imagine.

⌒

The letters began coming. He had turned eighteen not long after the trial, which had taken place so long after the event he hardly remembered much of it. Now he was an adult in the full sense. The letters were often scented. Women who believed they understood him, who reached out. His booking photo appealed to them, they said. He had looked strong during the trial, they said. They admired his strength, they said. They sent pictures of themselves. A few sent Bibles, which he threw away. He was mystified. He still didn't let himself think of the years and years that stretch ahead in this tiny room. He did not picture himself an old man, forgetting what it was like to have choices.

He could chase some thoughts from his mind, but he couldn't keep himself from endlessly re-looping those few annealed moments. At the trial, the commander of the SWAT unit that had stormed the school had said the total "incident duration," from the moment David had walked through the double doors to the instant in which they had slammed him to the floor, had been six minutes and eighteen seconds. That had shocked him, as it had felt as if it was hours. But really the memories were of four specific passages: The first shot. The first kid going down and not being sure if he was shot or diving for cover. Retreating; wanting to shoot himself in the boy's room and not being able to. Being surprised at the police wrestling him down and not killing him. Everything else was a haze. But those four moments came to him awake and in his dreams, vivid and relentless.

⌒○

One day at lunch, a fight erupted two tables away. The only real excitement in months. Who knew what it was about? The purported cause (some meaningless slight) was insufficient. The fight got so violent it spoke of years of deep and gathered resentment. Grievance hung in the air like the stench of rotten fruit.

Everyone went on lockdown. No TV, no music, no exercise. The computers sat unused and darkened. David sat on his mattress and again felt what caging was truly like, these moments with no outlet and the hours steeped only in one's own thoughts.

When the guard named Mason came around, looking through the slotted window at him, David begged him to break this torture. Mason says, "I can bring you something to read."

"Read? Read what?"

I don't know. There's magazines and some newspapers and some old books."

"What magazines?"

"I said I don't know . . . Sports Illustrated. Newsweek. I think they have Gourmet. And some yachting magazines."

"Yachting?"

"I don't know why either."

"Bring me that, then. I don't know why either."

But when Mason returned, he had bad news.

"Magazines all taken. Just some old books left." He held them out.

The books were all thick. David pointed at the thinnest of them. "Give me that one."

The book had a title he'd never heard, by an author he'd never known in all those interminable English classes. An old book, but the spine cracked when he opened it, apparently unread for all those years. It was a novel.

He read it. It was a story he'd never really known. It involved people who were neither fully good or fully bad, people who made mistakes and found moments in which they summoned their better selves. In this story, people changed, and sometimes learned. They grew; they knew sorrow and in time, some of them found joy. This was a hard story to follow, because it was not easy to reduce any one of the people in the book to a single, manageable dimension, as one could so easily do in real life. He thought of how little he read any books in high school, and how little anybody else did. It was a point of pride to get a high grade in a course in which you'd faked reading anything at all. But reading this book, with its muddy formulas and indistinct promises and confusingly complex people, he began to weep for reasons he didn't fully comprehend.

He thought then of being in the back of the police car, that car flanked by other police cars in a tight echelon, racing forward. The car moved in what seemed like endless acceleration, rushing him forward to his life of slow and endless days. He sat in the back with the handcuffs binding him behind his back. He could hear helicopters above him in the cloudless sky.

People were out along the sidewalks, their phones held in front of them to record this passage and post these on their feeds with various commentary and indictment. He was not invisible any longer. But he was reduced to being a single entity, the least of what he was. He realized, as well, that when the cars passed a bank, with its digital time-and-temperature, that first period would have only just been ending at school on any other day. He wondered how he'd changed now, exactly, and he had no answer.

"Why are we going so fast?" he finally said to the officer through the cage, whose hands were tight on the steering wheel.

"So they won't get to you and kill you," the cop said, his voice quavering. "The justice system will take care of that."

Here he was, then, like a node in one of his own games, the object of a search-and-destroy. He was the prize, the objective, the prestige. People had a reason now. The police cars rushed onward, their lights strobing all around him in frenzied announcement, their sirens a mournful chorus in five-part harmony, as he tried to imagine who he might have thought he actually was.

PART TWO

House of Sully

House of Sully

S pring of 1968, when change was lighting the sky and everyone was trying to hang on to something. The television
issues startling events, week after week. MLK had been assassinated in Memphis, in Prague the Czechs were poking the Soviet
bear. We were clearly losing the war in Vietnam. Men were getting ready for a journey to the moon. But in Dorchester, on
our shaded street, my mother's battle against change was more
delicate and resolute.

On our Saturday-evening excursions to restaurants we'd
long known, she railed against butter portions that now came
in little plastic squares with foil tops. "What happened to butter
pats?" she said, her bafflement turned on high. "What happened
to cloth napkins?" It wasn't just that these things had happened;
it was that nobody else seemed to be bothered by them.

My father, likewise, was more quietly perplexed by new con-
ventions, one of which was the credit card. He was a man who
kept his wealth in his hip pocket, a wallet which, when he was
paying for something, was produced with a flourish, a show of
currency being plucked from a deep reserve. I suspected part
of the disappointment of the credit card, other than what he
claimed ("It lets you spend money you don't have?") was the

muting of the gesture. Beneath the outer shell of fives and tens in his roll, there were mostly one-dollar bills, padding things out.

My mother, in that warming month, had decided she liked to look at houses, for no apparent reason. She said it relaxed her, a more amplified version of the window shopping she might have otherwise done at Filene's or the South Shore Plaza. And at least this way, she said, there was no chance of coming home with something we couldn't afford.

My father was perplexed. We were in no position to buy a new house. Yet he put up little argument. There was a lull to the household when she went out the door, redolent of perfume and dressed in a way she fancied sophisticated: a polyester suit and neck scarf. In her absence, there was a quiet in which household rules went into suspension, when I could carry food to the television and the volume could be put to levels I found more pleasing without the hushing and the lectures about the delicacy of eardrums.

My mother was a nervous type. She'd always been, but it seemed that when my brother was born—"The Baby," nearly age four now and wandering freely—she had become yet more troubled. She had smoked even more heavily during that pregnancy than I remembered when she was pregnant with my sisters; the cocktails had started earlier in the day. I knew we were not the most financially secure family, but the arrival of The Baby, the presumptive punctuation mark on the line of children my parents had produced, signaled a tipping moment. In due time, my mother saw a doctor about her nerves. She appeared to calm, more bottles appeared in the medicine cabinet, and then she would, in small iterations, begin to tense, to worry, and to quiet. She seemed in a constant wrestling match with her own serenity.

The house hunting really began the previous autumn with what seemed a propitious need: She'd been desperate to use a bathroom. We were coming up from my aunt's house out in the scrub woods beyond Carver—most of my parents' siblings had found their way to such exurban remove. It was a Sunday and we had gone after church, the only occasional visits that kept my cousins mostly strangers to me. On the road back up, my mother was sitting with The Baby on her lap, and she shifting under him. We were in the old '59 Plymouth Suburban, a rusty beast with the vague look of a rocket ship, with its fins and chrome. It was in bad need of a ring job; black smoke spiraled out the exhaust.

"What is it?" my father said.

She did not speak. Then she shifted again.

"Do you have to *go*?" he said, and she shushed him in a way that spoke of confirmation.

"I'll find a gas station," he said.

"I will not set foot in a filthy gas station," she said. "I can wait."

But five miles up the road, bouncing on old Route 27 with The Baby atop her bladder, she began to make long sighing exhalations.

We came upon a white colonial with the Open House sign on the front and cars lining the curb. My father drove past the house, letting up on the gas pedal and coasting by to limit the smoke issuing from our tailpipe. He pulled over, far up the shoulder.

"We can do this," my father said. "I have a tie on."

My mother turned and glared at me. "Watch The Baby," she said.

I could see up through the roadside trees a bit, and kept watch. My sisters crawled to the back of the station wagon and went to sleep on the blanket that was always spread there. In time, my father stood on the lawn with whom I presumed to be the owner, a graying gent who lit and relit his pipe while they spoke.

When my parents came back and got into the car, my mother looked deeply refreshed. My father started up the car looking glum, a bit guilty. As we rolled on home, one of my sisters said from the back, "I have to go, too."

"You can wait until we get home," my mother said, dreamy from her own release.

⌒

The Baby was *strange*—the word, in those days, for when an infant was stand-offish around people he didn't know. But he was far more than a baby now. He was a little kid who didn't talk much and always seemed to be racing from room to room. He couldn't sit still, lest he was staring into the color pinwheel of after-school television. The Baby was the ultimate afterthought. My mother had two miscarriages between my younger sister and The Baby, hence both surprise and a sizeable age gap. The Baby sometimes came through the room and stared at our father, and sometimes crawled up into his lap. But the little man was pet-like, an adjunct, someone who wandered unsteadily among our troubles and preoccupations.

The Baby was a climber. He was forever moving upward,

Careless. On bookshelves, porch railings banisters, He seemed to find his comfort up high. We had to be careful about open windows because we'd find him out on the porch roof, sucking his thumb and looking down upon the neighborhood like a gargoyle.

"What is this kid, part monkey?" my father would say, apparently oblivious to his own genetic predispositions: He was a house painter. In deference to The Baby's roaming, he put woodscrews in the window frame to limit how far we could open the second-floor windows, making the house all the more stuffy.

My younger sister, Ellen, seemed The Baby's surrogate mother, pushing food at him and wiping his face. Our actual mother was in her own place then, but even in a better frame it was tough for her, spreading out the love. On the long family drives we all paired in the station wagon, parents in the front, boys on the back seat, girls cross-legged in the backspace of the vehicle, watching the road recede and usually getting carsick.

The old car had no seat belts ("options," my father said derisively of the efforts of salesmen to get at his money), so my job was to throw my arm across The Baby's chest at any slam of the brakes, which, with my father, was often. He braked on intuition as much as on evidence. When The Baby had really been a baby, "car safety" meant rolling him on his stomach on the vinyl seat and pressing on the small of his back so he wouldn't plunge into the footwell, as my father, perplexed by a yellow light, would first surge, then reconsider, and finally stomp the brakes to come to a stomach-throwing halt about four feet past the stop line, nosed into the intersection.

The pictures of my mother from that year I was born were of her younger self, her happier self, stuffed into a cocktail dress with her stomach bulging with me, cigarette in one hand and highball in the other, mugging for the camera, and my father behind its viewfinder. He was likely laughing as well. But my sense was even then that she might have been in search of something, and maybe it wasn't particularly definable.

So my mother went house hunting. She'd dress in her Sunday best and after church she'd take the keys from our father and pull the '62 Impala wagon (my father replaced our car every three years, each vehicle equally out of date) from the driveway. The *Record-American* classifieds were spread on the seat with red-penciled circles on the houses across the Boston area, and the Texaco map smoothed beneath. No one was allowed to join her. She'd return late in the day, the look of relaxation palpable, the stack of flyers and mimeographed spec sheets folded into her vinyl purse. We were skeptical.

"There is such a thing as just looking," she said. "It's not like we'd ever move. But an open house is an open house."

Sunday afternoons, with our mother out, likewise relaxed everybody else. We would watch TV with our sneakers up on the coffee table; we would eat what we wanted. The house quieted down. Our mother would come home looking as if house shopping was deliverance. Her eyes, those days, were calmed. She'd go upstairs and lay on the bed and look as if she were sleeping, awake. House hunting's tonic effects could not be denied.

My father stood for hours by the window on those Sunday afternoons. I said to him, "Dad, can you just stop that?"

"Stop what?"

"Looking out the window."

He turned to me. "And do what instead?"

"Anything," I said. "It's causing me problems." The problem was the neighbors didn't like him watching them. The Waters family had just moved to the house across the street, the first black family in our neighborhood. My father made them uncomfortable, peering. Their son had told me, not in a particularly friendly way, and asked that it stop.

My father, at the window, seemed off somewhere. My mother was out looking at houses, but he was farther away.

"What problems?" he said.

"That's not important."

"Tell me," he said, as if he was trying to focus.

"Just never mind!" I said, stalking off.

⌒

That Monday morning, as I wandered down the stairs and then stopped, I heard my father talking in the kitchen. It was in that tone that was reserved for the absence of listening children. So I listened. My mother was scraping away at the eggs, tired as she always was that early.

"We really can't afford to move," my father said.

She didn't answer.

"It doesn't seem to make sense to look if we can't actually do anything."

She scraped at the eggs.

"Isn't it a form of dishonesty to take up their time when you know you aren't really a buyer?"

The spatula banged the plate as the eggs were served.

"Where do you tell them the husband is?"

I could hear her turning on the faucet. The pan hissed as the cold water hit it.

⁓

My father, in his house-painting whites, was truly the palest man on the planet. He had the kind of Irish complexion that suggested a thousand years of drizzling winters. He burned easily and on the ladder he used no sunblock, declaring it something for women and babies. By June he'd have acquired a kind of high scarlet on the nose and cheeks that looked painful but to which he claimed to pay no mind. Sometimes, when his nose began to peel, he'd put on a paint-splattered Red Sox cap as his one concession.

Standing in the window watching the neighborhood Sundays, he was like a wraith. The days all seemed like high dudgeon, unseasonable heat too early, boiling gray clouds roofing the city with foul mood, and on the ground the simmering of neighbors, of classmates. My mother's house hunting went into full gear. We'd all come home from Mass and immediately shed ourselves of our "good" outfits, hanging them carefully back in our closets, while my mother went right back to the car and headed out, as my father cracked his first beer of the day and began to edge toward that window, waiting for something, nervous-seeming.

When she came back, it was the one time of the week she

was really relaxed, somehow, from looking at houses in impossible price ranges. The papers she left on the car's floor held the circled names of towns I'd never seen: Wellesley, Newton, Sudbury. My father, one Sunday night near dark, went out in the car with his flashlight to look at the odometer.

Monday nights at eight, my siblings and I gathered at the television to watch *Rowan & Martin's Laugh-In*. My parents disappeared when the show came on, my father to the cellar and my mother to the bedroom, but with the windows open and the springtime air still, we could hear the neighbors' booming laughs from across the street, timing almost perfectly with the jokes we heard from our own television.

The weather seemed especially hot for late spring. Midweek, I played church-league baseball, for St. Ann. My family was not sufficiently upscale Irish to be at St. Brendan's, where they played out the oxymoronic idea of being "better Irish." St. B's was a place where you were expected to drop a five in the collection plate instead of a one. There was, to my father's view, an unmistakable haughtiness to those who joined St. Brendan's.

That night, when I came from my game, my mother was gone and my father was at the window.

"Where's Mom?"

"House hunting," he mumbled.

"During the week now?"

He let out a sigh, as if explaining to me was a chore. "She said she needed to. There was an open house in Allston."

"Allston? I thought she wanted to move out of the city."

My father turned and his look was blank.

"You'll have to ask her yourself," he said.

He waited a second more, and he said, "Things just keep changing."

⌒

Another pleasure wrought of my mother's absence was watching television at night with the lights out. She was convinced that doing so would ruin our eyes. She insisted, whenever the television was going, on countering its threats with all the lights in the room turned on. But here in the dark, I stared at the box in total absorption.

But as the show went to commercial in a fade-to-black, something did seem wrong with my eyes. For just that moment, my mother's warnings seemed realized as my eyes throbbed with color.

I felt in an instant as if in some fugue, the colors shifting before me. I blinked, then blinked again. But I realized what I was seeing was light on the walls, blue and pulsing, which caught me and pulled me away from seductions of the television. When I looked out the window, I saw a Boston Police cruiser with lights turning, and then I saw that my mother was sitting in the back seat.

I could see the neighbors looking out the window through their curtains as the police car idled, the mirror of my father looking out ours. The police had been kind enough to put out their flashing lights when my father, on the front steps, had asked them to; my mother sat in the back seat of the cruiser, like a queen waiting to be announced.

The cops stood at the door and spoke to my father. He spoke back to them almost in a whisper, and when he nodded they walked back to their car. They brought my mother in, one cop on each elbow.

It was the Boston Police, and one of them said, "Sully, if she'd gotten caught outside the city limits, you'd be bailing her out of jail instead."

Then my father took my mother up to the bedroom and they shut the door behind them.

⌐⌐⌐

Parents think they keep things from their children, and never do. My sister had been at her bedroom window, nearly directly above the porch, her hearing apparently sharpened in the pump of the moment. She had shrouded herself in the drapes and listened, about our mother going to the open houses, and excusing herself to use the bathroom, and going through the medicine cabinets looking for the pills. A real-estate agent, no stranger to the tattered threads of intrigue, had noticed this apparent inability of my mother to ever hold her bladder nor to ever make an offer on a house. On this evening, in Allston, certain people were lying in wait.

My mother had been getting away with it for months, two or three pills from each bottle, Valium and Librium and Dexedrine and Benzedrine, for which she had apparently tapped out her own prescriptions from our skittish family doctor. He'd told her that being a little blue after having a baby was understandable, but it was a long time now and that she had to cut back. In her travels, she gathered the pills in a small coin purse that, when opened, was as kaleidoscopic as the jellybean jar she displayed in the kitchen but didn't let us help ourselves to.

My mother stayed in her room for two days without coming out. My father hovered in the kitchen, ashen, but none of us was foolish enough to ask him what was going on. He made toast and tea and carried it up to the room, but he retreated as quickly, grave and stooped.

It wasn't so much about consumption, I thought; my parents were happy to drink, smoke, and eat to excess. It was about illegality. A police car on one's street, with one's mother in the back seat, was a life-changing happening. There was in my parents' lives a hard line between right and wrong, something church-taught and informed by the fiery lick of consequence. She had acted as if she aspired to better places but brought herself, and us, lower than we already were.

We children weren't supposed to know, but, as always, we knew. We observed them both in near-clinical distance. My father, in time, looked almost relieved. He abandoned his window post and seemed to find his greater comfort in the cellar, under one bare bulb, cool in the summer as the heat increasingly blanketed our neighborhood, and through the open windows the Waterses seemed ever closer.

I knew that the Waterses knew. Mr. and Mrs. Waters seemed imperceptibly more friendly; their son, Robert, seemed imperceptibly more removed. My mother stayed in her room all the more, acting as if none of us knew what had happened. She announced one morning at breakfast that she'd decided there was no point in thinking about moving, and our house here in Dorchester suited all her needs.

"We're here, in this house," she said. "For all its creaks and drafts, it's the life we have, I suppose."

⌇

June. School wasn't over, but it felt like the bottom of a hot summer. I tried to accept that there would always be people who didn't like me. I had the first pangs of attraction to a girl I knew would never be attracted to me. And, unable to find another job, I began working hours for my father painting houses.

Finally, I got bell-bottoms. A pair of green gabardines, the first bell-bottoms in the family, which represented the intersection of a) my mother's growing acceptance of what she considered subversive fashion and b) of the rapidly dwindling subversiveness of the fashion in question. The salesman at Filene's had actually bridged the difference when he said, "Oh no, these aren't bell-bottoms, these are *flares*." As long as that worked for my mother, it worked for me.

My father looked at my new pants and said, "In the Navy, they give you them for free."

"Those aren't the right kind," I said.

"There's a right kind?" he said. He shook his head and pointed out he was afflicted by "fashion delay."

"Just when I start liking something it goes right out of style," he said. "In the forties, I dressed like the thirties, and in the fifties I dressed like the forties. I just can't catch up!"

"Obviously," I said.

I wore those new pants two out of every three days, then four out of five, then five out of six, dropping them down the laundry chute from my room on the third floor. I receded back into my straight-legged chinos on the one day a week the bell-bottoms went through the laundry, always with one ear cocked toward the tumbling drum, waiting to resheath myself in the only mildly fashionable article of clothing I'd ever had.

My mother began to voice her concern about my overreliance on one pair of pants.

"You can't be wearing them six days a week," she said. "They'll fall apart."

"Why?" I said. "I'm getting your money's worth for you."

"But it makes us look like people who can only afford one pair of pants for their son."

"And possibly one pair of underwear," my father added. "People would infer."

"So buy me another pair of bell-bottoms," I said.

"We don't have the money," my father said. "We can only afford one pair."

"I don't really care what people think," I said, but of course wearing the bell-bottoms daily was very much about caring what people thought. I just didn't care what people thought about my parents.

My father's disappointment with people was deep and obvious, and nearly rueful. It seemed to my teenaged mind

unbecoming, that at his advanced age of forty one he hadn't
found his way to being *cool*, despite my own boiling adolescent rages. He had been in the War and there were times when
I heard him say, to my mother, "I risked my life all for these
assholes?" He was speaking then of just about everybody. The
world had closed in on him that much. The tone seemed one of
being stunned.

I theorized that being a house painter gave him too much
time to think. I also presumed that thinking, really, was the last
thing he actually wanted to do.

I'd previously worked for him a couple of times when one
of the other guys hadn't shown up, and it was an arrangement
that made neither of us happy. I tended to drip, even despite my
careful scraping of the paint-loaded brush on the lip of the paint
can; when I raised my arm to brush at a high target, the paint
ran back down my hand, veining my forearm.

"That's losing me money," my father would say, and go back
to his silence. Soon enough he demoted me. "Working your way
down the ladder already," he said, leaving me as the setup man
down on the ground.

I wasn't sure how he could stand it, up there in his own head.
Even fierce concentration on the painting still left too much
brain room. Things rattled around in there. I traced the many
twists of our family's life to those silent brushstrokes, the man-
tra of the roller: We did odd vacations, ate experimental foods
combined on the grill (clams with slices of banana, grape-jelly-
coated brisket), and listened to the ever-gathered lumber of his
mind. When he thought of old times, he put around those events

a shiny shrink wrap, both preserving the event but distorting it. The silence led him to new places, and old, and I think when he fell into certain somber actions, when his breathing became deep and regular as it more typically does in sleep, and when the paint roller could open speed on bare wall like an accelerating car, that he thought of the war he wouldn't tell us about.

My mother, after the night she came home in the police car, closed herself into a quivering fist. She shook while she made dinner, and took up cigarettes again. But otherwise she was stoic, which was how it all worked. The notion that we would have a "family discussion" about what happened was beyond possibility. She simply made it through days and lay on the bed more frequently, and with greater duration. Her daily habit rose from a half-pack, to a pack, then a pack-and-a-half, and the smoke seemed to bind with the rising humidity to create a kind of indoor smog we all passed through.

The house was a chamber of unholy vapors, which wasn't noted by anyone but gave the place the inverted sense of sacramental incense. We were all cleansing for what came next.

⟳

One day, my pants went missing. I went through the basket of clean laundry left on the second-floor landing, and then checked my closet, knowing my mother no longer ventured up to my room, in what was a negotiated agreement that involved me eventually returning the plates I'd brought up from my nightly raids of the kitchen. The pants simply were not there.

I immediately suspected a plot. I believed she'd really never approved of me wearing such pants, and my six-of-seven-day rotation meant that my habit, to use a phrase she applied to a lot of things, "had gotten out of hand."

Then they suddenly disappeared, and she was blaming me. The charge was negligence of the most self-defeating kind.

"You beg and beg for these . . . *trousers* . . . and now you've lost them?"

"I didn't lose them," I said.

"Did you leave them at your friend's house or something?" she said.

"And walk home in my underwear? How would I not notice that?"

"Did you ruin them and you don't want me to know?" she said. "Did you spill something on them and throw them in the trash?"

"Are you ashamed of bell-bottoms and don't want to admit it?" I shot back. "Did you throw them away because they're too cool, and then claim I was the one who's at fault? Are you that incapable of changing with the times?" She looked as though she'd been slapped, in my blunt indictment of her incorrigible squareness.

We receded to opposite reaches of the kitchen, like boxers returning to their corners. My father said, "Just keep looking for the damn pants."

And I did. The disappearance represented the first time I actually didn't trust my mother on something. I congratulated myself on that suspicion being a mark of my rising adulthood. The illusions were being cast off. I told my friends that my mother had stolen my bell-bottoms as some sad inability to evolve, and, of course, it got right back to her, as other mothers among us likewise struggled with these odd and vaguely threatening articles of clothing. The lost gabardine bells were grudgingly replaced by a pair of stiff, straight-legged Levi's, which were marginally agreeable to all parties. I pulled them on and staggered around like a man in twin stovepipes. They would soften, in time, to something reasonably hip. But I didn't completely regain my trust in my mother after that.

It was, strangely, the neighbor's voice that I remember that night. A throaty scream, let out and as quickly contained, no more than a second of sound. But I remember it still. We awakened, sitting in our beds, listening. Then, nothing. We all leaned to the windows in the small hours of that early-June night, and maybe, because of what we all were but did not claim to want to be, we wondered what mayhem was ensuing across the way.

Sitting in the dark at 3:30 on a Wednesday morning, we waited still for something: sirens, or crashes, or someone running from the house. We peeked through our shades and saw their house lighted in every window. When I came down the stairs, telling myself I was just looking for something to eat, but knowing I was burning with curiosity, I wasn't surprised to find my father at the window, in his boxers and undershirt.

"What are you doing?" I said.

"Shh," he said. "I'm just concerned."

We stood silently and watched from our darkness. There

wasn't a lot to say. An hour went by without a sound, but the lights blazed at the Waterses' windows, with no apparent movement from within.

"Don't you have school in a few hours?"

"Yeah."

"Then get to bed."

He knew I would stay up as long as I wanted; he just didn't want me standing there with him. Of course, real neighbors might have gone over and asked if everything was okay, or phoned out of concern. We and the Waters family were not real neighbors, but rather ragged edges of two different worlds, bumping up against each other like the tectonic plates on the earth science test I had in the morning, and for which I should have actually studied for.

〜〜

That morning I walked to school in what seemed like such odd quiet that I had the abrupt seizing feeling it was Saturday, and that I had somehow forgotten. My feelings were only confirmed when I reached Dot High and it was locked tight. *What the hell?*

I wandered back, still fairly sure it was a weekday, and went to a *Boston Globe* newspaper box on the corner. There was only one newspaper left lying flat at the bottom of the box, and I strained against the glass to see it. I was more confused because it said Tuesday. I was pretty sure the day before had been a Tuesday.

Back at the house, my father's van was parked in front of the house, and he was sitting there in the driver's seat, like he was waiting for something. He had left for his job while I was just coming out of the bathroom, but now he was back. I walked back up to him, about to ask, but he put his finger to his lips. He was listening to the radio. When he seemed to be sure he could, he spoke.

"They shot Bobby Kennedy," he said.

Bobby was shot, but not dead. The TV went all day. He'd just won the California primary, a process about which I only had vague understanding; now he was in surgery "fighting for his life," a phrase the news anchors used over and over. We were all in a paralysis, hovering. My parents sat on the couch, drinks in hand, staring at the television even as little new was reported.

It hadn't even been five years since President Kennedy, but I'd been too young to absorb that. It was scary for me in the way ten-year-olds get scared. But the event did not speak, then, to the kind of complicated, fractal webs of evil I now knew, as a fact, to lurk out there in the darkness. I was fifteen and it was very clear, in a way that left me shaken and furious. We had just gotten over Martin Luther King in April. Now it was our house, and all the others on the street, that stayed lighted into the late hours. And there was no mystery as to the killer. A Jordanian, which had its own sense of surprise: I'd thought of places like Jordan and Syria as only a wisp of history from the dry Bible readings in our overheated Sunday Masses at St. Ann's.

That day seemed suspended, as if we were simply forfeiting. I don't remember eating; my mother took a carton of Kools and the last of the Dewar's and went to the bedroom. I tried studying on my bed and instantly fell asleep.

My father stayed up with the radio and at near dawn he came to my room and said "Are you awake?"

"Yes," I whispered.

"He died," my father said.

"Okay."

"Go to bed then."

"I am."

"I mean go to sleep."

"Okay, I was."

He went down the hall and into the bedroom and shut the door. I waited for sounds in the night but none at all came.

～◌

My father was a house painter, and therefore an acrobat, hanging on one foot on third-floor ledges, brush in one hand with the other gripping a crumbling drainpipe, defying gravity and yet making this wherewithal into just another prosaic day. I assigned him no points, because up there, like Daedalus on his waxen wings, melting in the Dorchester sun, he was always about to plunge.

He seemed fearless with heights, clambering skyward, and didn't seem especially careful. I alternated between being certain he couldn't possibly stumble and being certain that his days would end with a three-story swan dive onto a Dorchester sidewalk. When he got up there by himself he seemed to get dreamy, the hand sometimes pausing at mid-brushstroke as if he was working through something in his mind. I'd stand below, watching errant paint blobs spiral down on me as if white rain.

My father's stabs at theological inquiry tended to dead end.

"I try not to wonder too much what's out there beyond," he said, "because it makes me not want to paint houses."

We, at our age, objected to this kind of talk because what we required was that he just keep doing what he was doing, quietly. We just wanted our parents to continue their dull lives, to lock into an existence we saw as their due, so that our successes would stand, contrapuntally, like a slap of color across an expanse of gray-primed clapboard.

Another house on our street went on sale; another white family moved out, another black family in. The new people, the Robersons, came to our door before they went to the Waters house, in what seemed a strategic approach. Mr. Roberson had just moved the family up to Boston from Nashville; he was an actuarial at the Hancock. He spoke with the quiet voice of subtle confidence and had the measured tone of a man well versed in tables of probability. I looked at him, like Mr. Waters (who was a lawyer), as a man higher in station than my house-painter father, coming into our neighborhood because, for some reason, it was the next ring beyond Roxbury's solidarity. The Robersons were young but heavyset, which made them look older, more substantial.

Mrs. Roberson was a round and laughing woman, and my mother, chatting there on our front porch, seemed to take to her. But no invitations were made, no further courtesies extended. They lived far enough down the street so as not to change much at all, except for that little tilt of color. We heard of some black families a few streets over; them, we never saw. We were in the littoral zone between Roxbury and Southie, and the swirl had begun.

"The race thing confuses everything," my father complained.

"Are we being normal by ignoring our neighbors, or are we racists without knowing it?"

⌒

My father couldn't believe we were worried about what black people thought of us. "I thought it was about us accepting them," he said. ". . . which of course I do . . ."

My father's view was that because we were decent, welcoming, nonjudgmental people, the idea that our new neighbors the Waters and Roberson families would see fit to pass judgment on us was unacceptable. In his mind, we were being "mighty white about it," another phrase that must have once meant something less volatile. My sister Jeannie rolled her eyes.

"Please don't take that talk outside the house," she said.

"He already has," I said.

"How so?" my father said.

"Dad, when you stand on a ladder against the side of a house and talk loudly enough for me to hear down on the ground, the echo off the side of the house sort of . . . broadcasts it . . ."

"Dear God," my mother said.

"Who do you think knows?" Jeannie said.

"Everybody knows," I said.

⌒

On a particularly hazy Monday, a man came knocking on our door. It was late afternoon and my father had just come in from a job. The man on our front step was black, well dressed, and fairly young. From his place on the welcome mat on the porch,

118 / EDWARD J. DELANEY

which was as far as he was allowed to get, he told my father he
wanted to buy our house.

"This is going to be a black neighborhood now," the man
said. "I'll give you fair money before the value drops even more."

"Drops?" my father said. "What are you talking about?"

"The value of your home," the man said.

"I still pay the same mortgage every month," my father said.
"The bank hasn't told me anything about the value dropping."

"You see, in another six months, with the blacks moving in,
your house will be worth half."

"I'm happy to pay half the mortgage," my father said. "I'll
call the bank and tell them a young man on my porch says—"

"No," the man said, "you don't—"

"Let me call the bank," my father said. "I'll get to the bottom
of this."

The man didn't know whether my father was joking or not,
and neither did I. My father stood there staring a moment, and
the black man said, "You can see that the neighborhood is changing. You're going to want to move soon."

"We're out of the house-hunting game," my father said.

"It's going to be a black neighborhood now," the man
said again.

"I have neighbors," my father said. "I like them just fine."

"They may not like you so much."

My father looked over his shoulder at me. "That's what my
son tells me," he said. "It has something to do with my personality."

"I can see that," the man said, not smiling.

"Well, we're staying here anyway."

The man turned and then turned back,

"We'll see if you're saying that in a year," he said.

⌒

My father was unusually quiet that night, despite my mother's prodding: *Are you all right? Do you have gas?*

He was keeping his own counsel, but holding it in with visible discomfort.

"I'm thinking," he said.

"About what?" my mother said.

"Man stuff," he said.

"Pardon me for asking, then!"

He ate silently and chewed unusually slowly. My sisters just stared at him; it was only when he was talking that they paid him no attention.

My mother just stared at me.

"What?" I said.

"Why isn't he speaking?"

"I have no idea," I said.

My father took his fork and with a theatrical ponderousness laid it across his plate.

"What do you want to *speak* about?" he said.

"Anything," my mother said.

"Let's talk about how school is going," he said to my sisters, who groaned in unison.

"Tell me what you learned today," my father said to Ellen. "Tell me anything you learned."

"Thanks, Mom," Ellen said. "Really."

Later that evening my father sat in his chair, not even energetic enough to spy on the neighbors. My mother gave him room, busying herself in the kitchen. My father's desire not to lose value in his house was likely matched exactly by his desire not to be told what to do. He had left the military with a life's dose of taking orders, he'd said, which is why he'd always been self-employed. He had a contrary streak you wouldn't see right away. It was all hidden under his constant stabs at conformity.

The same young man came back again on the following Tuesday, smiling, solicitous. He was ready this time and he wore a yellow bow tie.

"I thought I wasn't seeing you for a year," my father said.

The man laughed heartily.

"You never told me your name," my father said.

"It's Washington," he said.

"Well, that figures."

Mr. Washington stopped smiling only for an instant. Then the corners of his mouth widened again and he just kept on.

"And you?"

"Call me Sully."

"That figures, too . . ." he said. "*Sully* . . . Let me guess, that's short for Sullivan?"

My father said nothing.

"I can tell you're a man who won't be fooled," Mr. Washington said. "I can tell that the usual pitches won't work on you."

It seemed to me as if this itself was the usual sales pitch, but my father's shoulders relaxed.

"I think of myself as a problem solver," Mr. Washington said. "A friendly party, if you will. We can all see what's happening with the city and I think that if we do this thing right, you, myself and the potential buyer will all benefit."

My father waited for more.

"Now let me tell you what I think you're thinking," Mr. Washington said. "I think you're thinking, 'I like my neighborhood and I want to stay right here.' But that's the exact problem. The neighborhood you like is evaporating. There aren't many days left where things can be like they are. Change, decay, unhappiness. *Conflict.*"

"So you have that low an opinion of black people?" my father said.

"That's not what I'm saying."

"But it seems pretty obvious you are."

My father said quietly he wasn't interested in hearing all that. Then he just swung the door closed.

"You just shut the door in the face of a black man?" I said.

"I just don't need to hear all that shit," he said to me, brushing by as he headed for the cellar.

⸺ ⌒◡ ⸺

Air-conditioning would eventually change the way summer privacy worked in our immediate neighborhood. Air-conditioners cost $200 then, and while I would never have had the guts to ask then, I've guessed since that my father probably made $100 a week. Our house was a creaky and high-ceilinged echo chamber, which, with the counterweighted windows pushed open, became absolutely megaphonic. And I knew so, because coming down the street from the baseball field, I could hear my father's voice, wafting down the street like the tang of cooking onions. Most times, thankfully, he was saying nothing meaningful.

So it was to our surprise and dismay that it was the Waters family that got the first air conditioner in our neighborhood. A delivery truck pulled up, and the sweating fat man pulled out the cardboard box clearly marked GENERAL ELECTRIC, FASHIONAIRE, and 8000 BTU. We watched from our house as the Waterses' living-room window opened and the unit was pushed through, settling with a resonant clack in what made me think of the lunar module docking with the Apollo capsule. The fan of the unit spun up and the affirmative roar of moving parts and of bad air expelled made the Waterses inaudible to us, and we to them.

Then, in the next week, three more units, smaller ones, appeared in their upper windows, which truly seemed distressing. It was one thing for the parents to have their room cool, but the children, too? That was unthinkably beyond us.

"I thought heat didn't bother black people," my father said.

"Dad, come on," I said, although I was more at ease with the Waters sealed in their air-conditioned living room.

"If my schooling serves," my father said, "black people come from Africa, and the South, both known for being damned hot."

"I don't know about that," I said.

"It's those of us with the ancestry from Ireland who can't take summers like this," he said, "Our people lived their lives with clouds and dampness. That's why we sunburn so easy."

"So buy us an air-conditioner," I said.

"Forget it," he said. "It's not just the thing itself, it's all the electricity it would take. Jobs are down for me."

"Maybe we can just run it when it gets really hot."

"We only have fifteen-amp circuits in this big old barn," he said. "Turn it on and we're blowing fuses all over the place."

My father said, with finality, "We just don't have the power to be cool."

∽

July

"Is it possible you can pull a muscle in your back by having pants that are too tight?" my father said. He was walking gingerly, and indeed the trousers were testament to his refusal to surrender to his expanding girth. He claimed he ate no differently than ever, and when my mother suggested perhaps his metabolism had changed and he should modify his diet, he said, "Why in God's name should I live with less?"

He also wondered, aloud, why we should sell the house. My mother called back, "Don't!"

My father had long ago stopped calling our house "The Sullivan Compound." He had stopped after JFK was assassinated. It wasn't funny anymore. The irony he had imbued into what we were, and what we were not, had only lasted for a while.

After JFK was killed and the neighborhood began changing, he started up with "Casa Sully." But in time he moderated it.

"House of Sully." I imagined a unique coat of arms that included paintbrushes and beer cans, crossed ladders, and the rising flame of a summer grill.

House of Sully was a chipped-paint hulk, our equivalent of the shoeless cobbler's children. It was, in my mind, as much a given as the sun rising over Squantum on long days. Anyone who would presume to buy it was simply a barbarian at our gate. Our house had been bought from an old man who had died after three decades of no improvements. My father had originally pledged to rebuild it from the bottom up, but after some cursory work, we'd gone forward as the neighborhood's nominal eyesore.

But Mr. Washington returned to our front door a month later, smiling still.

"Just who the hell *are* you, anyway?" my father said.

"I'm just a simple businessman," Mr. Washington said.

My father gave him the Stare.

"I am able to see how things are forming," Mr. Washington said. "It's a matter of speculative negotiation."

My father stood his ground.

"No one's doing anything but trying to help all involved," Mr. Washington said.

Then a curious thing happened.

"Hey!" Mr. Waters shouted from across the street.

Mr. Washington turned and looked, the smile fading.

"Well, Hello, brother," he said to Mr. Waters, who was advancing with an unmistakable glare.

"Don't 'brother' me," Mr. Waters said. "Stop bothering my neighbor."

"What do you mean, friend?"

"Don't 'friend' me, either. We don't need you and your tactics. We don't need you trying to chase away people who've lived here just fine for years."

Mr. Washington's smile had gone to a smirk now, and he said, "You *want* to live in a white neighborhood?"

Mr. Waters fixed his look and stayed silent.

"Brother too good for the ghetto now?" Mr. Washington said, his composure faltering.

"Young man," Mr. Waters said more evenly, "every one of us was supposed to be too good for the ghetto."

The summer went hazy and when you looked across the harbor, the horizon was no longer distinct. The daily creep of humidity made life feel soaked and slowed. I was glad baseball was winding down and I knew it would be my last time in a uniform. I'd have liked to have been better at sports, but I was not. I lacked both strength and coordination. Pitchers in the church league were throwing the most rudimentary kinds of curveballs, but they badly confounded me. Another of the things I accepted in that summer I was fifteen.

The war was on every night on the evening news. Walter Cronkite and those big glasses making streaks when the studio lights reflected off them and into the lens of the television camera, something like lightning bugs that flitted over the hedges in the last wisps of dusk. He spoke of Vietnam.

War had a way of suddenly insinuating itself, not so much on the news, or on the television shows like *Combat,* but at moments that you couldn't prepare for. My father's van was acting up, so one morning we went by the A. C. Smith Service Station in Quincy. He knew people there; one was a mechanic who came bobbing out on crutches. It took me a moment to register that his left leg was missing, all the way up to the hip, the leg of the green work pants rolled up and fastened with a diaper pin.

"Sully, whaddya got?" the mechanic said. But before my father could really explain, the man was under the car on a dolly, clanking around with an adjustable wrench. I was staring at the one booted foot coming out from underneath, something like Oz's wicked witch under the house, until my father shoved me.

"Show a veteran more respect than that," he said.

It was twenty-three years after the Big One. We the children thought of this as something awkward and annoying about our fathers; every time somebody mentioned the War, it was as if we were supposed to say thank you. Twenty-three years made the whole thing moot to us. Our crew-cut fathers. These men negotiated civilian life with something they'd kept from the experience, not the old uniforms as much as the way they came at life, the way each man in his home got to be the General, and the way a military regard of order always seemed the ideal imagined for us, the children, if not the practice for them, the fathers.

We reconfigured all that as a case of being "uptight." Where they sought order, we sought "freedom." My hair was getting longer now and I waited for my inevitable cease-and-desist orders, along with those issued on the subjects of sleeping late, sleeping on my stomach, eating all the food, drinking all the milk, using too much toilet paper, and generally acting sullen. But in the midst of assaults of all kinds, this lesser insubordination of my hair had been overlooked.

My father was constantly worried about ticks. He seemed obsessed with them, and when he came in from painting houses he spent time inspecting himself. My mother largely didn't believe ticks were a problem, arguing that they were representative of some larger malaise that was affecting his thoughts and mood. She'd never once had one affix itself to her person, nor to her knowledge had a tick ever glommed onto my father's pasty skin. He explained that fact by noting the effort with which he avoided them.

My father was of the mind that my mother's refusal to take ticks seriously was representative of some withdrawal from the facts of the natural world. The idea of the city, of its pavement and right angles, had taken from us all a real understanding or appreciation of the sinister incursions of the world. We had too much control, he said. Water leapt from faucets at the turn of a handle; heat could be summoned at the push of a thermostat; throw a switch and there would be light. This all worried him. He worried we didn't understand the ravages of life.

Ticks seemed shorthand for the nearly uncountable ways misfortune could come upon you. When my sisters came in from the park, he would check their hair as he might have a dog. These unseen invasions, he said, would make you sick and weak and vulnerable.

My father's sudden-seeming focus on things nearly below the ability to see struck me as a from-the-ground-up reassessment of his fears. Things had gotten too big, too complex.

"The War," he said, "That was easy. Hitler. That's how easy it was. Pearl Harbor. That's how easy it was. All this stuff? Vietnam? I don't even understand it anymore."

He seemed to keep trying to simplify the events of the day. Martin Luther King's death wasn't the result of white supremacy, or Jim Crow Southerners, or of the cloying discomfort we might have all had. It was just "some nut." Same with Bobby. "Just some towelhead nut."

"I don't think you can say that word," my sister Ellen said.

"You can't even say *towelhead* now?" my father said, utterly mystified.

⌒

Things were changing almost instantaneously at Dot High, but the whole world at that point seemed in the midst of instantaneous change. Things were tipping everywhere. Congress had passed the Fair Housing Act that April; suddenly the white enclaves, like the McCormack and Old Colony housing projects in Southie, and all the public housing of Charlestown, were mandated to throw open their doors to black people. As they did, maintenance stopped and the places slowly began to die. Although in Dorchester people seemed to quietly note Dot High was already integrated as Southie High was not, that summer we found out the Boston School Committee had come up with a new plan.

Dot High, seemingly overnight, was going to become a mostly black high school.

The fundamentals of this had an air of the sleight of hand, but of course any magician will tell you it's really the long preparation in hidden rooms that allows for the illusion. It tracked like this: In the spring of 1968, the School Committee had decided that certain high schools should be changed from tenth-through-twelfth grade into ninth-through-twelfth grade. I had entered Dot High as a tenth grader, and the previous summer we got the letter that there would be a ninth grade at the school.

But the real trick was this: For whatever reasons of design, the mostly black neighborhoods had "middle" schools that went to eighth grade. In the white neighborhoods, there were "junior high" schools that went to ninth grade. The school board decided anyone coming out of middle school would go to a nine-through-twelve, and anyone coming out of junior high would go to a ten-through-twelve. It seemed like a delayed reaction that everybody seemed to suddenly figure out that nearly every new student arriving that fall at Dot High would be black, and that this was going to be both ninth and tenth graders, and in three years or so the whole school would be overwhelmingly black.

The reaction, then, was fury. Whatever racial anger simmered beneath the Dorchester collective psyche now seemed poised to burst. Through the summer, I heard how one of my classmates or another who would be leaving the high school and enrolling at one of the Catholic schools nearby: Boston College High for boys, Monsignor Ryan for girls, or maybe all the way to Archbishop Williams in Braintree or Matignon in Cambridge, depending on where your father worked. Fewer and fewer of us staying on at Dot High were white.

The high school lay at the west edge of Dorchester, bordering the black neighborhoods of both Roxbury and Mattapan. The paper said we'd have about seven hundred black kids enter the school, and it was noted we had no black teachers, something that implied a needed, immediate change. When I saw Billy O'Connell out on the street or down at Kelly's store, he repeated everything he had heard, and it was all bad, and I suspected at least some of it was true.

I waited for my parents to say something, but they said nothing. It was a given that we didn't have enough money to afford even Catholic school. In retrospect, I don't even know what I expected them to say.

We watched television, secretly sure there would be another assassination. It was part of the way things were now. School was starting in a couple of weeks and more of my friends were transferring to the Catholic schools, which were mindfully silent on the situation that was bursting their enrollments with new tuition, and that it wasn't for the religion. I'd been confirmed by Cardinal Cushing two summers before, and all I could remember was the ritual slap of the face, how it came at me weak and clammy, like a wheeze of death slipped through the doorjamb. The nuns at Catechism had told us it might sting, but the Cardinal shook as he stood before us. Catholicism to me seemed similarly ghostly and cold, not so much eternal damnation as eternal insinuated disapproval. The Catholic Church was like my mother, forever proclaiming catastrophe, but in practice more inclined to nervous worries and trivial preoccupations.

The weather was a gray blanket of humidity and I wondered about school. Rain spat but didn't seem to gather, adding to that pall of forestalled relief. In the summer I was now largely friendless with the conclusion of baseball; we were at that age when we were too old to play games and too young to drive, and we had tired of just hanging around on the corner watching cars go by. When we were in school, I had at least the connection of shared boredom with others, but this was a summer of staying in our rooms, brooding, thinking about girls whom we could not approach. I heard somewhere that Sabine Fitzpatrick, my crush, was now dating Danny Malloy, a guy with access to his father's car, a convertible '65 Buick Special. I could never compete with that. Even when my time came to drive, I'd be choosing between a Chevy Impala wagon and a panel truck. I felt the pinch of constricted destiny.

The Russians were massing at the Czech border. Everybody waited for the next bad thing to happen, although my own anxieties were far more personal. I wandered down to Kelly's store just to see who was around, and all that was there was Brian Toole, likewise drifting. His face had, since the end of the term, exploded into constellations of acne, and his voice had suddenly gone deep.

"Where have you been?" he said.

"You mean today?"

"No, generally. Are you leaving the high school?"

"No. You?"

"No."

Toole looked as if he'd also grown a few inches since I'd seen him last. "Then we're screwed," he said.

"We'll be all right." I had no idea if we would be, but I always felt a natural impulse to contradict Toole.

⌒

August.

My father said once, "Every day of my life has become the struggle against the fact I have no apparent talent."

He hadn't chosen house painting. It essentially had chosen him. His affinity to it had mostly to do with not being afraid of scaling high and rattling ladders. He did the job with no scaffolding, no safety equipment, and no apparent caution. And I still regret these years later that never once did I have a pang of fear that he might not come home from work one night.

My father could hot-connect 15-amp circuits with his bare hands, claiming it didn't hurt even as the sparks spat from his fingertips. But he'd be rubbing his palms against each other for a couple of hours, and sometimes after wiring a circuit his speech was slurred for a day afterward.

There were many things for which he had no fear, sandwiched among his many discomforts. He said when he went to Fenway Park, even that limited crowd made him feel tiny and forsaken.

"What's the living population of the world?" he shouted down from his ladder. "Three billion and some?"

"No idea," I shouted back.

"Half of that is Chinese, and they're godless. That's still a billion and a half of us left, desperate to be noticed. But that's just the living. How do we rate? How do we think we're even being seen?"

We all were invisible, in our own ways. I floated, not sure anybody much cared what I had to say; my sisters were invisible to me then, simply strangers in the household to whom I assigned little attention. There was some recognition of them all when they were tying up the bathroom, yapping at the dinner table, or eating food from the refrigerator that household custom and hierarchy would reasonably entitle me to. They began to further irritate me when I began to worry about my return to Dot High.

"What are you, a racist?" Jeannie said. "Why are you so afraid of black people?"

"Children don't understand the complexities," I said. "You have no idea of what I'll have to deal with."

"I'm thirteen, you know," she said.

"Exactly," I said.

It was all easy when you were in the seventh grade. Everybody was harmless. There was a certain amount of softness, the last laugh before the absolute hell of high school. Besides, the changes had not yet reached such a point in the elementary schools. I also secretly suspected my parents were hoarding their money to send my sisters to Catholic high school.

I just waited.

"I did a lot of embarrassing, ridiculous things that are so alive in my memory they make me cringe thinking about them," my father said. "But most of those are left only in my head. The people who might have known have forgotten those things that I remember. It's a long-lost memory to them, but it eats away at me.

"Thankfully, the real bad memories die with my parents. My advice is, make your mistakes while I'm alive, so when I die you can be done with them."

"I wish," I said under my breath.

I wished, but only rhetorically. I wished he would just stop talking like that, and therefore end the continuation of memory. That he would be a new person. I didn't really want him to pass in the literal sense. In truth I couldn't imagine it. He hung off that ladder and he slapped the paint and head-butted the low sky. He argued about God, I thought, because he was way up there, forty feet closer than me to the firmament.

"I have no gripe with dying, some day," he said. "But it is not convenient at the moment. Your mother needs to get groceries every week for you people."

The "you people" thing was becoming a problem. He'd said it for as long as I could remember and applied it to any multiple of humans not himself. My siblings and I were "you people." My uncles and aunts on my mother's side were "you people." I think it went back to some military thing, but then there was the August morning he shouted across the street to our new black neighbor, Mr. Waters, as he stood in his dark suit hosing down his small lawn, "So you people prefer air-conditioning?" I think he was trying to be friendly, in the wake of the Mr. Washington situation. But I saw Mr. Waters's shoulders drop, and then he just waved and nodded and went to turn off the spigot.

My father happily drove off to work, and Mr. Waters likewise slid into his Cadillac for the ride into the city. He was some sort of lawyer; neighborhood talk suggested he might have once been a Freedom Rider.

My father's seeming obliviousness worried me on two levels. One was whether a remark like that might blow back on me, and hard. The other problem was the fact that I was indisputably his son. As he sometimes said, when I tried to argue I was nothing like him, "You plant beans, you get beans." I was getting more worried that, despite my self-styled sophistication, I might be genetically predisposed to make such mindless mistakes.

⌒

My parents were still young, but I don't remember them that way. They seemed ancient to me at fifteen—he was forty-one and she was forty. In my house, The Baby still careened through rooms, and my sister Jeannie was getting louder and more opinionated.

Jeannie had latched onto my rising anxiety about the resumption of school, and in turn I was finding her extraordinarily annoying.

"You're just mad because I'm a teenager now, too," she said at the dinner table. "You're not so special anymore."

"When was I ever special?" I said.

My father took on a look of suffering. "Look, neither of you is special . . . does that settle it?"

My mother nodded. "He's right," she said. "All of you are exactly the same." Jeannie smirked at me, victorious.

It was easy for my sister to hack away at me, but my father had his limits, especially in the way she questioned everything now. She began an inchoate narrative about how we didn't have air-conditioning due to my father's inability to get beyond house painting.

"Well, I'm working my way up the ladder," he said, spooning his peas over his flaked potatoes. When she said nothing, he turned to me and said, "She doesn't even get it."

"I get it," Jeannie said. "It just wasn't funny. But I'm in my room at night dying of heat stroke."

"She's going through the change, is why," my mother said to no one in particular.

"That is just gross," Jeannie said.

"Yes, it is," I said.

"Why don't you all gang up on me," Jeannie said. "I'm just making the point that if you could earn more money . . ."

My father pointed his mashed-potato-encrusted fork at me. "If this one can pick up the pace, maybe that would happen."

"Oh, so now it's my fault," I said.

"Yes!" they all said, as a chorus.

In early August, in Miami, Nixon was nominated at the Republican National Convention. My father saw him as the same pathetic also-ran JFK had beaten years before, and refused to take him seriously.

"It solves one problem," my father said, watching the convention from his chair. "At least it'll be two guys running for president who say they want out of Vietnam. The problem is, I just don't believe Tricky Dick."

The war had been hanging over me with each passing year, getting worse and worse, seeming more intractable. It was looking to be in my future. Everybody was tired of it but no one had any idea what to do. As my bow-tied tenth-grade history teacher, Mr. Sheehan, had said more than once, "America has never lost a war, and it's not going to happen in some Stone-Age Asian swamp." It wasn't immediately apparent that this thin and balding man was an ex-Marine who had stormed the beach at Saipan, but he had the medals to prove it and kept them on his desk, facing the chair where a student would sit when the student wasn't measuring up to simpler challenges, such as homework. Mostly, Mr. Sheehan spoke of the war in Vietnam indirectly, teaching and quizzing us about wars that had mattered, wars in which we had a moral purpose, wars in which the enemy was more formidable. Clearly, he noted, America pulling out of Vietnam would be akin to the shame of our football team failing to show up to play South Boston High. When he put it that way, it seemed that we did have to keep fighting until the bitter end.

With RFK dead, we were waiting for McGovern to be nominated, but afraid he might not win. I was fifteen and following politics not only because I was not far from draft age, but because it now always seemed as if the next one was going to get shot to death. Could somebody really assassinate McGovern? The fact was, it felt nearly imminent.

At Sunday Mass, my father listened intently to the gospel reading, but tended to ignore the homily. He said he liked a good
story more, and an opinion much less, and the gospels were a
puzzle unto themselves. He said if you read the Bible carefully
enough, you could defend almost any point of view.

That steaming morning in that airless church, they read
Mark. The story was of Jesus at Bethany being anointed by a
woman, using expensive oils, and the complaints of his followers
that the oil could have been sold and the money used to feed
the poor.

The reader, Mr. McGee, was a man who had once complained about my father's trim work, a truly unforgivable sin.
He was in his stiff suit, and he leaned into the microphone at
the lectern: "And the Lord said, 'Why do you trouble her? She
hath wrought a good work for me.'"

My father shook his head, which made me hold my breath.

"And so it is written," Mr. McGee said, shutting the Good
Book emphatically.

My father, with The Baby on his lap, snorted, and people
noticed.

"Works for Him, I guess!" he said in the Irish whisper. The
old lady in front of us turned and gaped at him, and my father
looked at me.

"I guess this guy Jesus never made a bad call!" our father
hissed.

Me, sitting there entrapped, whispered, "I don't know anything about that."

"He always got to be right, and you know why?" my father

said, setting his eyes now on my sister Jeannie, "because he didn't have any *teenagers* . . ."

On the way home in the car, our mortified mother did not speak.

"Hey, if I can get away without expensive oils, so can this guy," he said, seeming to think he was trying to make it better. He was speaking of Christ Our Lord as if He were the "this guy" on the next barstool.

"And these priests," my father said. "Vow of poverty, my ass. Old Shaugnessy drives a Lincoln and eats at the Red Coach Grill three times a week. Poverty like that, I can take."

Where my father was a skeptic, my mother was someone who still was trying to respect the rites. She became offended at what she saw on Sunday in church, the declining standards, in such a way I began to think her gravestone epitaph would be HE COULD HAVE AT LEAST PUT ON A SPORT COAT. My father wore a suit every Sunday, the same suit all twelve months, the donning he referred to as "my weekly embalming."

"Jerry, you talk too loud in church," my mother said.

"Amen to that," my sister Jeannie said from the back.

"Double Amen," Ellen said. My father glared at her through the rearview and said little the rest of the day.

⌒

My mother began trying to get out of the house, but my father was always leery of where she was going. She needed, she said, to connect with people outside of the family. She needed to talk.

The question of whom to connect with left her searching.

Most women she knew were bogged down with family, most with more kids than our modest four. There were a few divorced friends, but my father remained hesitant about blessing that.

"I have to get out of the house once in a while," she said. "Just for a bit." She knew what we were thinking.

"Maybe Helen," she said.

My father nodded. Helen—Mrs. Dunn—was very vocally "on the wagon." This lent a notability about it, as the idea of airing out such personal failure had not nearly yet become fashionable. She was in Alcoholics Anonymous, the proclamation of which my father noted as defeating its own purpose. "You know, most people actually prefer the 'Anonymous' part," he said. People trying to drink less in those days never saw it as a virtue, more a failure. They usually faked it with club sodas and cherry-garnished ginger ales so no one would catch on. And given the amount of drinking the "normal" adults did on a regular basis those years, calling oneself an "alcoholic," or going to AA, was a move that had to have been accompanied by the litany of vomited-upon rugs at holiday parties, pissed pants, various car wrecks chalked up as "falling asleep at the wheel," and diverse statements and disruptions, all of which were very much on Mrs. Dunn's neighborhood rap sheet. My mother's own house-hunting "incident" was also on that widely-followed-but-unwritten ledger as well; Mrs. Dunn had come with cookies a few mornings after my mother was brought home in the police car. Mrs. Dunn was summarily rebuffed at the door by my father. "They're like a damned cult," he said.

But now, my mother was better, only taking the various pills prescribed her and no longer, we presumed, rifling through the medicine cabinets of strangers to effect further relaxations. Being now limited to four separate prescriptions—for Darvon, Equanil ("For ladies in distress," one of their ads had read), Quaalude ("For a good night's sleep"), and Serax ("Freedom")—and having resumed her chain smoking, my mother was back to normal. But she had to get out more, she said.

So it was probably with some surprise that Mrs. Dunn answered the phone to find my mother thanking her for the cookies, these months later. A lunch was arranged, not in Dorchester but over at the Red Coach Grill in Braintree. I knew its hushed air-conditioning and its red-leather booths; I wondered what Mrs. Dunn drank in lieu of the hard stuff. Shirley Temples, most likely, in a shroud of cigarette smoke.

My mother went off in the car while Jeannie and I took turns watching The Baby. He and I sat with our feet in the kiddie pool to cool down, and when my father's van pulled up just a few ticks after noon, Jeannie had a peanut-butter-and-jelly sandwich waiting for him. My father opened a beer and ate his sandwich in the shaded part of the patio, silent.

He had another beer after that and headed back to his job, just shaking his head. The Baby ran up the stairs to watch him out the bedroom window, then ran down to the cellar, then ran into the kitchen.

In the living room, I turned on the television. *It's Happening* was on, as was *As the World Turns*, and *Let's Make a Deal*. I chose the last of these for its noise and movement, hoping The Baby would come in and be ensnared. But I heard him pounding up the steps to the third floor. The echo of his movement was like a day-ghost that haunted our meditations and reveries.

On the television, Monty Hall was holding his microphone to a woman in some kind of farm outfit, haggling over a $199 Hotpoint refrigerator. But I knew I was listening for other things, and in time I heard the slam of a car door and my mother's footsteps. I heard her go through the kitchen and straight up to the bedroom.

My father's van came back into the driveway just before three, as the credits for *The Dating Game* were rolling. He was home way too early. He came in the kitchen and took a beer from the refrigerator and sat silently at his place at the table. I moved from the couch to turn the channel to *To Tell the Truth*, feeling trapped at my station. The Baby wandered into the room and sat next to me, glancing into the kitchen where our father sat, too soon, too silent.

My mother came down from the bedroom a bit after four, probably to figure out what to make for dinner. Her footsteps padded down the stairs and then into the hallway, then stopped at the edge of the kitchen.

"What are you doing here?" she said.

"Too hot out," my father said. "How was lunch with Helen?"

My mother considered this question, then waved him off.

"I liked her a lot better when she was a drunk," my mother said.

⌒つ

There were many mornings of my youth that I awoke to my father's voice, from behind the bathroom door: "Who moved the damned plunger?" (And upon his exit from the bathroom, his usual benediction of "Let us spray.") The house was hardly majestic, but when you lived there you really saw its little problems and its disrepair, as we could see it in our family itself.

"We can never sell this house because it wouldn't be fair to who bought it," my father said. "There's something wrong with everything." The house was old enough and big enough to have the curiosity of an old laundry chute, at the bottom of which was a perpetual sedimentation of our filthy clothes, always queued for a cycle of washing and drying that never seemed to catch up. We'd listen at night to the loose change clacking in the drum of drying laundry, like a ritual drumbeat.

Then one August night, the smiling Mr. Washington showed up once again at our doorstep. The Waterses were not home, and Mr. Washington seemed to know that. He was in his seersucker, with a thin bow tie and his summer hat in his hands.

"How are you, my young friend?" he said in his crisp business voice when I came to the door.

"Fine," I said.

"Is the man of the house available?"

My father was already there, looking at him through the screen.

"I can't believe you're back," my father said.

"I did so with knowledge of the change at the high school this fall," he said.

"What change?" I wasn't sure if my father knew or whether he just wanted Mr. Washington to say it out loud. I never knew when my father was playing dumb.

"The changes in what we might call the 'racial composition,'" Mr. Washington said. "Is your boy going to the high school this fall?"

"He sure is."

"Then I hope he's prepared for what awaits him."

"Why, what awaits him?"

Mr. Washington laughed, as if he was being put on.

"Your boy may find himself with troubles. From the blacks."

"What kind of trouble?"

"There can be violence in these situations."

"Are you saying black people are violent?"

"Oh, no, no, no . . . I'm not saying that at all."

"Well, you can't be talking about him being violent," my father said, motioning to me. "I mean, look at him."

"Hey," I said.

"It's just that tensions can rise in these, well, mixed situations," Mr. Washington said.

"So you're for segregation?" my father said.

"No," Mr. Washington said. "I'm just for people living among their own kind. Not by law, by choice."

"I don't get it," my father said.

Again, Mr. Washington took his business card and slipped it into the gap of the screen door. "I can give you a price for this house if you want to talk more," he said.

"Who do you represent?" my father said. "This card only has your name."

"No one at all," Mr. Washington said as he headed to the

street with a tip of his straw hat. "I'm an independent businessman. Working for the people."

⌒

My mother made her second attempt at social flight on a
Wednesday, when she joined the local chapter of what my father
referred to as "The Ladies Club." Its real name was the National
Organization for Women, but my father could never seem to
remember that. "Women's Auxiliary," he said.

She dressed much differently for this meeting than she had
for the house-hunting adventures. She seemed plain, bordering
on severe, far from how she'd dressed even for lunch with Mrs.
Dunn. In fact, she was in the kind of getup that if my sister
Jeannie had worn it, my mother would have called "just not
very pretty."

Again she got in the car and drove off into her mysteries.

⌒

That Wednesday night, August 21, the news came that the
Russians had stormed into Prague. The Czechoslovak leader,
Dubček, was being reported as dead. We'd followed the movement from the spring and it had felt exciting, the throwing off of
the tyrants. And then, that was that, as if it had all been strung
out like a joke. I lay on top of the blankets listening to the WBZ
radio man repeating the same information over and over. Here
and there, a small bit more would come through. People were
in the streets, fighting. I felt it, even as I had nothing specific I

could fight for on any given day. I was a teenager, pushed by the things happening around me, getting up in the morning to see what new calamity had now happened. And now it had.

⌒

The matter of school clothes was upon us. It was my mother's tradition to take me to J. August in Harvard Square to select a "main outfit." J. August was as fancy as my mother could imagine or my father could afford, a definable notch below the Andover Shop or Brooks Brothers, which, as my mother pointed out, "aren't for Catholics anyway." On our list were three button-down shirts and two pairs of khakis. Underwear and other nonvisible attire could be gotten at Bradlees, or some other similarly downscale chain store. And, thus, we returned to the matter of trousers. In Chicago, the Democratic National Convention had just been descended upon by bell-bottom-wearing hippies, setting my sartorial case back significantly. The Yippies were nominating a pig for president. My renewed fashion campaign—to not return to high school looking like one of the Four Freshmen—was being ruined by these people.

"Troublemaking pants," my father said, ruefully.

To get to J. August, my mother and I did our rare subway trip, boarding the Red Line at Field's Corner and riding silently to Harvard Square, emerging at the news kiosk for the half-block walk to the shop. This was a trip repeated yearly since I was seven or eight. We'd once thought it an adventure. We'd have lunch or stop somewhere in the Square for ice cream. We were no longer like that.

My mother was in no mood for arguments. I was still nursing my incontrovertible conclusion that she'd thrown away my bell-bottoms and pinned the blame on me as a ruse. She knew I thought that, and though I said nothing, she would sometimes see what I was thinking and say, "That's really just ridiculous." In turn I wanted to scream, "Then where are they?" But even as we trundled on the T across the city and river and toward Cambridge, bell-bottoms were now apparently a non-starter.

In the shop, I was tape-measured for a shirt and then I tried on chinos, the proprietor neatly marking the cuffs with his bar of soap. The pants seemed to have just a whisper of flare, J. August's stiff nod to changing times. All around the Square, Harvard summer students wandered in massively wide bell-bottoms, tie-dyed shirts, and flowing hair, a happenstance that seemed to go unnoticed by my mother. I was outfitted as if I were, in my father's common phrase, "wearing a dog-crap suit to a horsefly party."

My father and I sat down that night to watch the Democratic National Convention in a way one might have *The Friday Night Fights*. We had soda and popcorn, and The Baby had his Mallo Cups (my brother remains to this day the only individual I've ever known personally to favor Mallo Cups when any other candy was available). Violence was in the air. Mayor Daley had said the Chicago police would make sure things proceeded in an orderly fashion.

"Yeah, orderly like the First Armored Division," my father said.

Jerry Rubin said the Yippies would "Do what we want, when we want to."

My father said, "Give them a reason."

And so, like an athletic event, I knew which team my father was rooting for, and I and of course we were in opposition. As we watched footage of the Yippies camped out in Grant Park, my father said, "Look at them all, in their ridiculous bell-bottoms."

"Didn't you wear them in the Navy?" I ventured.

"Sailors wear bell-bottoms for a reason of utility," he said, confirming nothing about himself. "It's for rolling up the cuffs when they're swabbing the deck. These people look like they haven't seen soap and water in their entire lives."

That night, despite the Yippies outdoors, the action was taking place inside the Chicago Amphitheatre. When one correspondent mentioned that one could smell the nearby Chicago Stockyards, my father said, "It's not the cow shit you smell, it's the hippies!"

"What are you so mad about?" I finally said.

"Me? I'm not mad about anything. Okay?"

"Okay."

"So watch the convention," he said.

"I am watching it," I said back.

"You're watching history," he said.

"That's what you always say."

"You and your causes," he said. "Last week it was Czechoslovakia, now it's the Yippies."

"It's all important."

"You lose interest, though," he said.

"I have things to worry about in my own life."

"Do you even know what happened to Dubček?"

"He's dead."

"No, he isn't."

"Dad, he's dead. You need to follow the news more."

My father shook his head at me, dolefully.

"What other things do you have to worry about in your life?"

"Lots of things."

"Like what?"

"Like going back to school."

"Yeah, so? I hated going back to school, and look what happened to me."

"I thought you said house painting is an honest trade."

"I did. The problem is that most honest work doesn't pay much."

"Oh."

"Does that help you understand about school?" he said.

"Yes," I said. I didn't understand at all, but I just wanted him to cease. Our conversations made me anxious. I realized then, as we fell back to our silence, that he actually thought we'd just had a father-and-son.

⌒

Dubček, it turned out, had survived. He'd been taken away to Moscow the night of the invasion and when he returned to Prague on the twenty-sixth, things were done with. With the fact that Dubček was alive, I was nearly disappointed, a martyr taken back from me. School was less than two weeks away.

The revolution was seeming over and everything seemed to settle into a drab silence, no news and no change, just back to the way it was. Humphrey got the nomination in Chicago, and he did not strike me as being anything like Dubček.

And I was waiting to return to a high school that would not be the way it had been when I showed up as a tenth grader a year earlier; suddenly, it seemed, I was going to be in the minority.

I began to consider my options. I'd turn sixteen on the last day of November. I was anticipating, with that, my first true degree of freedom. I knew I needed to think ahead, because no one else would do that for me. Then, just as we got in that last stretch of dog days, my mother announced she wanted out of the marriage.

⌣⌐

September, then. Why are the memories of my youth so humid? There were clearly springs, and falls, and winters. I remember being under the blankets in my drafty winter room listening to the radio broadcasts of the Bruins, WBZ 1030, as Bobby Orr turned up the ice with the puck on his stick. I remember clumsy touch football on cold grass and falling leaves. I remember shoveling snow on bitter mornings, my father watching from the window with his coffee. But somehow the 1960s remain with me most as hot nights in a house with open windows and no breeze. It was the heat under my shirt and the mint of my Irish sunburn as I endlessly stared into the cold maw of our rattling fridge, seeking sustenance.

The first day of school was hot like that. My skin chafed

under the just-unwrapped shirt. I'd pulled the pins from it, feeling its sandpapery hand, knowing it would be as uncomfortable as everything else that day. The smell of my paper lunch bag and my new books was nauseating. As I made my approach to the school, I was seeing how the numbers had fallen in, and the numbers were not looking good for me. From the newspaper, I knew the school had expanded, over the summer, from 960 students to more than 1,300, but droves of white kids had been pulled by their parents. Firsthand, everything felt suffocating. The walk down the corridor was a bang of shoulders, the din of slamming lockers. I kept my head down, all the way. The new students looked as unhappy to be here as we were, all part of a great social experiment.

One can ponder the notion of integration and racial equality, but for us it was present in three harsh dimensions.

And there was Billy O'Connell, looking pale, coming by me as if we were strangers passing through a foreign land.

"I can't believe you're here," I said.

"My parents can't afford Catholic school," he said, his voice trembling, at least in my estimation. "Look at all this . . ."

"So what do we do now?" I said.

"I'm sixteen in five weeks," Billy said. "And the minute I am, I'm quitting school."

"What will you do then?"

"I'll get a job or something."

"You're going to be a *dropout*?" That word was not one you threw around, but that's how dire the moment was.

"Who cares?" Billy said.

"You don't think we need to finish school?" I said.

Billy swept his arm at all that was around us. It's not that anyone was really bothering us; they were simply having nothing to do with us. We were now the minority. And that, it turned out, felt very small.

"Well, I'm sixteen in three months," I said.

I hadn't been thinking of dropping out before this. But right now, this first morning, I had to look at the situation for what it was. I wasn't athletic, I wasn't good-looking, I wasn't really that good in school. I wasn't especially tall or strong. I wasn't much of a conversationalist. I wasn't especially funny.

And now, worst of all, I was white.

⌣

"I never get past two hands," my father said, sitting in the yard drinking a can of Schlitz. "I count the days I've gone without the beers and it feels good to get to one hand, then maybe a hand and a finger, and if I'm really good, a hand-plus-two. It's been years since I got to two hands . . ."

"That's not good, is it?" I said.

"Well, it's not as if I'm an alcoholic. I just drink too much beer."

There was a day when I suddenly noticed his gut, the stoop in his shoulders, the gait. I'd never thought of my father as young or old. He was just a grown-up. My sudden scrutiny of him may have been linked to my sudden preoccupation with my own physical changes. Unmistakable signs of sideburns had coalesced along my ears. A wisp of mustache was visible in the mirror, if one shined a strong enough light on it. I was changing. It made me think of everyone now in more dynamic terms.

⌒つ

In the way matters were settled in those days, my parents attended to their business as if we children did not actually live in the house, or had much a right to know anything. Somewhere that late summer, a discussion was effected; my father wandered out to his van and drove away; it was only after three or four days that my sister Jeannie said at breakfast, "Where's Dad?"

"Your father has moved out," my mother said, pushing the eggs around the pan.

"We did kind of notice, you know," Ellen said.

We waited, but my mother said nothing. She seemed utterly emotionless.

"So what's going on?" Jeannie said.

"What's going on is times are changing," my mother said.

"That's not good enough," Jeannie said. "Where is he? Why is he gone? What did he do?"

"He didn't do anything," my mother said evenly.

"Then he left us?"

"I don't want to talk about it."

"Dad walked out on us?" Jeannie said, her voice rising.

"Why do you care?" I said to Jeannie. "You barely talk to the man."

Jeannie looked at me with clear disbelief.

"He's my *father*," she said.

"Oh," I said, "now he's your father."

My mother turned to me with a look of calmness I found disturbing. "Things change," she said.

"Yet I still don't have bell-bottoms," I said.

I could think of no place he could be staying other than at my grandfather's new apartment, but that was all the way down in the Lower Mills, and my legs were not used to such exertions. But I think my anger was giving me a second wind. I had not been to my grandfather's since we had moved him in after my grandmother's death.

His apartment was wedged into the basement of building owned by a fireman he knew. The house was a wooden triple-decker and the bulkhead had been replaced by a more proper covered entryway. There was a doorbell now, three steps down, but the place was so small I elected to knock. I heard a surprised kind of shuffling within, then my grandfather's reedy voice, asking who it was.

"Jarred," I said.

He opened the door and said, "What's wrong?" Behind him was the smell of cigars and casual flatulence.

"Is my dad here?"

My grandfather's face was a mask of alarm and confusion.

"Is he missing?"

"No, Grandpa, he's not missing. I just can't find him."

I was aware of the alcohol on his breath, strong. He was not the clean-shaven, coffee-drinking, doughnut-bearing man I knew from Saturday mornings.

"Why can't you find him?" he said.

"My mother said he doesn't live in our house anymore."

My grandfather drove a 1962 Dodge Polara he'd just bought. It had a push-button transmission, in an apparent nod to the Space Age, but he was a man of simpler times and his hand constantly went for where the shifter had been on his last car, a deep muscle memory he could not shake. We began crosshatching the narrow streets of Neponset looking for the telltale van. My grandfather did not talk, nor ask; he seemed deep in troubled thought. Finally, he said, "There was a time when a man who brought home steady pay was a king in his castle."

I nodded.

"Providing he didn't hit anybody."

He waited then, and I realized.

"No, he never hit anybody," I said. "Not even me," I added, to further emphasize my father's evident self-control.

My grandfather had been a pressman at the *Boston Evening Traveller*, but had retired the summer before, when the *Boston Herald* bought it out. Back then, the paper landing on your doorstep was something like political registration. But now the *Traveller* was gone, and the *Record* had merged with the *American*. People were reading the papers less. I wondered if the news of the world was just too trying for average people. Despite my grandfather's decades in the pressroom, he apparently had never followed the news very much. Now, clearly, less so. He seemed burrowed into his apartment, an old man not all that old at sixty-two, but seemingly at discomfited rest. In the car, he had an unlit cigar in his mouth, which his lips tumbled expertly, like a log roller.

I was swiveling, trying to see the van, less angry now than regretful I'd brought my grandfather into it. It would complicate things, and he didn't need bad news. I was surprised my father hadn't told him anything, but then again, I wasn't surprised.

"There," my grandfather said.

The van had two wheels on the sidewalk in front of a house, and the ladder rose up behind the trees. My grandfather parked, and we got out, looking.

My father was on the top rungs, with a can of paint hung in his elbow like a handbag, a rag rolled around the wire bail to keep it from cutting into his arm. He seemed as he always was, working away, thinking some apparent benign thought as his face, relaxed, caught the afternoon sun.

"Hallo," my grandfather called up the ladder. My father seemed to have a delayed reaction, realizing there was a voice. He looked down and saw us.

"What's wrong?" he said.

"Where have you been?" I said. My father looked at me like it was a trick question but then pointed a finger upward. "Right here on this ladder," he said.

"You haven't been home."

"Yes, I have. Didn't you hear me showering this morning?"

"I heard *someone* showering. But Mom said you aren't living there anymore."

"Yes, I am."

"Wouldn't Mom know if you're living there?"

"Well, I'm not *sleeping* there. But I shower there, and change. And eat. You get so fixed on that TV you didn't even hear me in the kitchen. Your mother's up in the bedroom talking on the phone with her new friends from the women's auxiliary. Last night I finished off the cheesecake."

"And I was blamed for that," I said, putting together the pieces. I had actually suspected The Baby. "Then where do you sleep?"

"At a secret location."

"You sleep in the *van*?"

My father shrugged. "It's really very peaceful."

My grandfather said, "Did she throw you out?"

"I wouldn't put it that way."

"How would you put it?" I said.

"I'd put it this way: Your mother is exploring some of these crazy ideas going around these days. Change is fashionable. I was expecting it for a while."

I walked to the van and looked in. There was a camping air mattress and a sleeping bag, and a cooler next to it, and many empty Budweiser cans. It did seem to suit him.

⌒

So the mornings now began with the sound of my father creeping up the steps in the pre-dawn, of showering, of rooting around in the refrigerator. My mother and sisters were late sleepers by nature, and people whom the alarm clock would need to ring hard against to rouse them. Sometimes though I would hear The Baby, up early, going down to the kitchen to sit with my father while he had his cereal, rinsed and reshelved his bowl, and made his sandwich. I'd hear a door gently shut; way down the block

I'd hear the engine of the van start up. This was how we lived now, and still no one was talking.

With my father haunting the premises, and my mother perched on the bed two floors above, the house had become a quieter place. No longer overheard through that door (as had often regrettably been the case in my pre-adolescence in the second-floor bedroom that was now The Baby's) were their restive love calls (Mother: "That was a little quick, wasn't it?" Father: "I had to hurry. My beer was getting warm.").

My mother was going to her meeting that night, which meant she left out stew that we would dish up ourselves. I hated my mother's stew, so I was eating a bowl of Frosted Flakes. The Baby had joined me, so I'd poured him a bowl as well. She came into the kitchen, smoothing her blouse and smelling something like incense.

"The stew is for dinner, not cereal," she said.

We kept eating.

"Maybe I'll give you the stew for breakfast, then."

She went into the refrigerator and extracted a Fresca. She appeared to not be eating at all.

"So what do you do at these meetings?" I said.

"Excuse me?" she said.

"These meetings you go to. What do you do at them?"

"We mix secret potions and cast spells on the men of the world," she said. "What do you think we do?"

"So by joking about it, you don't have to give me a straight answer . . ."

"Listen to Himself," she said, "deciding he can get mouthy."

The Baby looked at me, masticating his Flakes.

"I just asked you a direct question, that's all," I said.

She sat down at the table and looked at me so directly I looked back down at my cereal.

"We discuss the need for women to be treated equally, and how to implement change. We discuss the opportunities for employment for women on an equal basis—equal pay and equal work."

"Employment?" I said.

"Yes?"

"You want a *job*?"

"Why not?"

"Oh God," I said.

"What's the matter with you?"

"What about the food and the laundry? What about *him*?" I said, nodding at my brother.

"Jeannie helps with all that. Ellen will soon, too."

"But being our mother is your job," I said. "It's not the daughters' job to be the mother."

"Maybe piping down should be your job."

"What possible kind of work do you think you can do?" I said.

My mother got very quiet then.

"You're being extremely insulting," she said.

～

"I keep thinking about things that are all over," my father said from his ladder. "You kids never think that. You're happy to be done with being twelve and thirteen and fourteen.

"But I think, *I used to love that, but it won't happen anymore.*"

He wanted me to ask him what, but I wouldn't.

"Like knowing a girl might give you a second look," he said, his echo rattling the houses around us.

"Can we please not?" I said.

"Do you know any girls you even have a shot with?" he said.

"I'm not having this conversation."

"Well, that's clearly a no," he said.

I was not really wanting to have any conversation with him, but there was one I knew I wanted to have less. Which was that I was dropping out on my sixteenth birthday, not all that far away. I was in the habit now of coming around to his job after school, trying to figure out if he was coming back home or not. I'd look up at him and puzzle out why it mattered.

He, in turn, looked down and was puzzled by me, that I thought I had a right to opinions.

"Don't think you're so smart," he'd say. "Three years ago you were twelve."

"I actually don't think I'm so smart," I said. "I try to tell you that every time I get my report card."

"Is there some problem at school?"

"Not exactly."

"Is anyone bothering you?"

"Not exactly. I just don't feel comfortable there."

"Oh, now his highness isn't comfortable."

I knew that after every statement like that, he silently thought, *Try being in a war.*

And my discomfort really had nothing to do with the

changes at the high school. It was me. I was fifteen and, in that world, all that mattered was other fifteen year olds. The rest of the human race more like window dressing. Adults were of two types, benign and malignant. I went into to Dot High every day, feeling talentless and bored, and left there well reminded of both. Everyone else there seemed new, and didn't seem interested in anything I had to say. People walking by me on the street were just extras in my movie; old people were always old and the notion of my ever being anything but fifteen was difficult to absorb.

⌒

My father began showing up at the house when my mother went off to her now twice-weekly meetings, and things seemed the smallest bit closer to being back to normal. Wednesday nights, *The Beverly Hillbillies* was on, and he liked it because it made him feel sophisticated.

He parked his van on the next street over, so when my mother did pull in the driveway he could slip out the back. His retreat was through the cellar and out of the bulkhead, the hinges of which he had oiled to crypt-like silence. He seemed to get some sort of pleasure out of being so stealthy, never seen by my mother yet felt, like a spectral presence.

In the mornings I came down to find him showered and eating cereal, looking at me with blank eyes. He was staking certain corners, and his look said to me that he expected me not to tell. My non-response told him this was fine with me.

And after he had slipped from the house one morning, I

went to the cellar, where I found his new lair, the blow-up beach mattress hidden under a drop cloth he was apparently using for a blanket, and a winter coat rolled pillow-like behind that. That night, late, I lay in bed waiting for his nearly soundless entry into the cellar. That usually came just after eleven as my mother sat in the bedroom talking on her Princess phone. I assumed he'd laid over at the Hibernians lodge, a place where he always found refuge, and dubious counsel.

So he was, more or less, back in the fold after three weeks. I felt a relief. My mother apparently had not a clue. The joke was on her, even as my father lay his head down in the cellar darkness. But from here, he really didn't have to go much further. We could all live like this indefinitely, even if the world outside wasn't staying still.

⌒

And autumn, then.

"Can't you see how I can't go back to that?" my mother said after discovering my father's burrow, the way one might find mouse droppings near the furnace. "It's not about your father, it's about where I need to go in the world . . ."

I, for one, wasn't buying any of it. It all seemed at an impasse, with my mother now refusing to "backslide" into her marriage, and my father, now rooted out, turning our basement into something of a pad. He got a rug from somewhere, then a couch, and then a small TV, running the wire up to the massive antenna he'd years ago installed on our roof. He was starting to feel much too at home in this odd new space, and I wondered if, down there, his life was really all that different. In some way, spending his working hours on a high ladder, and then his leisure hours below ground, seemed to bring a surprising balance to him.

"Curious men are always the fornicators," my father said to me one evening.

"Uhh . . . okay . . ." I said.

That's Saint Augustine, for your information."

"Wow," I said.

"I mean, I do remember *something* from school. How do you forget a line like that?"

"I guess I won't, now," I said.

My father shrugged and worked on his sandwich. "The point is clear, which is why St. Augustine is still in print."

"If you say so," I said warily. I'd already noticed the book itself at the top of his basement pile. More shocking than anything that year was that my father was now reading.

The presidential election, by then, seemed foregone. RFK was dead, and that was pretty much it. Late that night, my father came up from the basement in clear defiance of my mother and turned on the television.

"Bring on the inevitable," he said. "Either one of them isn't ever going to be Bobby."

Nixon was always going to win, it seemed, and then he won. It was actually closer than any of us expected it to be. I didn't know who would be president until I got to school Wednesday morning. Some of the teachers conferred together, shaking their heads and saying it should have been different. This, after all, was Massachusetts.

My mother, like almost everyone else, seemed distraught by Nixon. It had seemed unthinkable that the old nemesis could actually come back and win, stepping over both Bobby's and Jack's graves on the way to the Oval Office. But I always saw Humphrey as a bit frightening, too. The earnest, ponderously foreheaded Minnesotan didn't seem right to end the war, and I truly needed somebody to end it before I hit draft age. I saw Humphrey smiling and wondered how he'd do; he struck me as the indulgent parent who wasn't up to the big tasks.

Nixon had promised to end the war, too, "But what do any of Nixon's promises mean?" my father said. And, he added, what kind of name was Hubert?

My parents struck me similarly, two parties campaigning for outcomes they might not have believed in themselves. Every day that went by without my father being served divorce papers was another day he could shake his head and say, "She doesn't even know what she wants!" Every day he banged nails in the basement let my mother observe, "He really doesn't want to go through with it." The impasse was there. Everybody hovered. The Baby was suddenly inclined to go prone, flopping on the floor in front of the television, glazed-eyed and clammy. Jeannie was mostly looking after him, other than myself, and he seemed suddenly needy. We tended to give him things to eat when he got that way. It began to show, too. My father observed that The Baby was "blowing up like a tick," perhaps a sidewise swipe at the state of the household.

Adding to my mother's sudden recurrence of malaise was the October marriage of Jackie Kennedy to Aristotle Onassis, someone largely agreed upon to be a filthy-rich thug with bad skin. It seemed deflating to my mother, that Jackie's Doris-Day-like single life had been snuffed like a church candle and a lost prayer.

"That man is hideous," my mother said into the phone, to whom I did not know. "And he's *short*. Who in God's name could love that?"

And then, even more cutting: "I actually thought she was better than that."

My mother retreated to her room, the bubbly crest she'd ridden in the fall diluted by the gray days of early winter. At the dining room table, she kept going over the *Life* magazine with the pictures of the Onassis wedding. Earlier, before she'd gotten to the magazine, I'd found in the same issue an article, with photos, about a movie called *The Killing of Sister George*.

"Suddenly, it's the thing," *Life* magazine said of homosexuality. *'Sister George' is the most explicit of a flock of films about lesbianism,* the heading said. Another reality I'd never considered, buffeting me; pictures of women kissing and rubbing each other's backs quickened my interest. I waited anxiously as my mother moped over the wedding pictures, but when I finally got to the magazine again, those pages had been excised by an unseen hand.

I was watching TV when my mother finally came down from her room. She went in the kitchen and fixed something for herself, and when she came in the living room I did not turn to her. I could sense her right behind me.

"Well, I guess we're all stuck here together," she said. "Forever."

"I guess."

"Maybe it's not the worst thing."

"I suppose that's something you have to figure out for yourself," I said.

"I just wanted something better."

"So do I, but when do you see me getting it?"

"You're a child."

"Keep telling yourself that," I said. "That way you don't have to care what any of us think."

She came around in front of me, half-blocking the TV. I didn't want to look her in the eyes.

"Well, what do you want? Don't you want to get out of here? It doesn't seem you're so happy with all this."

"I don't know," I said, resignedly. "Shouldn't you be talking to Dad about this?"

"None of this is really about your father," she said. "It's about me."

"Can't it be about us?" I said.

I still hadn't looked at her, but she turned and left the room. A few seconds later, I heard the bedroom door slam again, the dull toll of us being whole again, as we were.

But even as we held, we didn't. My mother had been putting out applications for jobs, and one day she was hired. My sisters seemed to fall somewhere between skeptical and elated about the news.

"What exactly are you going to do?" Ellen said.

"I'll be working on the switchboard at Bank of Boston."

"In the city?" Ellen said.

"Well," my mother said, "that's where Bank of Boston *is*."

We knew the usual arguments—who would make breakfast, who would wash clothes, get The Baby cleaned up and squared away—had already been made moot by her long languor and her consequent launch into her new life of feminism. And I was way too busy with this new way of life to even read *Lord of the Flies*, so I was failing that test for sure.

"Does that mean that you'll make more money and we can buy more stuff?" Ellen said.

"In theory," my mother said brightly, "that is something we'll be able to do."

That night, I found my father sitting in the basement. Even though he now had the run of the house, he seemed to like it down there.

"So here's the problem," my father said, sitting crosslegged on his basement mattress with a Miller High Life in one hand and a TV dinner in the other. "My crime has been my silence."

"You?" I said. "Silence?"

My father chuckled bitterly. "A silence of a crucial kind. One I learned from my own father. I tell you to break the cycle."

I was sitting on a paint can drinking a Yoo-hoo.

"So the lot of the husband is to bear criticism," he said. "That is a timeless truth. You bear it, you know? *Jerry, the toilet's clogged again! Jerry, if you don't put water in your cereal bowl after you use it, it hardens like concrete! Jerry, why can't you put down the toilet seat?*"

"I have heard her say all that."

"But the unspoken agreement is you don't do it back. You

don't say, *Kathleen, why can't you just be quiet while I'm obviously reading the paper? Kathleen, why can't you let me sit down for a minute before you're off about your day? Kathleen, if you're going to take an hour to get ready, just don't tell me it's going to take fifteen minutes."*

I did not speak.

"The problem, my son, is you do five things they make sure you hear about, and then they do five things you're too polite to mention, and they think they're ahead five to nothing!"

That seemed to be the extent of his resistance to the women's movement. As his resistance to our changing world was to simply escape up his ladders. I'd gone to school that fall and learned to accept things being different, maybe the one useful thing I learned that year. I made some friends, as that eventually happens when proximity to people you thought were unlike you is just another boring thing at school. I don't know that any of us saw ourselves as anything but people carried by a larger tide, even as we were part of it.

⌒

September 2001. My father's funeral was on the fifth of that September, a hot day in which the clouds stood high over the harbor and we sweated in the heat as they laid him down.

My sister Jeannie had the idea about the procession. If you didn't know my father, you might have seen it as sarcastic. It wasn't. His pallbearers were six house painters, and not in suits and ties but in full "dress whites," T-shirts and white double-kneed Dickies, spattered with their colors as soldiers are beribboned, the incidental camouflage of their trade. Six men, black and white, young and old, men he'd shared a living with, and a mission. In his later years he'd started hiring guys, the protégés I refused to be, and after they'd struck out on their own they had become part of what my father called the Sully Mafia, responsible for painting all of Dorchester, as he saw it. These were men who had, in their own simple way, set themselves to the task of changing the way our small world looked, even if hardly noticeable, even if in unfortunate colors.

My brother, Tommy—The Baby—had taken an afternoon off from his vice president job at a financial institution to go to the old haunts and recruit that honor guard. Mr. Donahue had suggested a final touch, and Tommy deferred. It sounds odd, but you had to be there. Mr. Donahue showed up with two empty cans of Sherwin-Williams Duration, the Dom Perignon of exterior latexes, and with his drumsticks (kept wrapped in a handkerchief since V-J Day), he beat out a solemn funeral march as they hoisted my father, in his box, up into the church.

At the gravesite, two sailors arrived in a government car and stood at attention throughout. So he really had been in the Navy! One sailor played taps on a bugle; the other one saluted, and as he did, a small tear formed on his cheek, as I saw one forming on the cheek of Mr. Waters.

The Waters family had remained our neighbors until Mr. Waters retired and they went down to Florida; for three decades they had stayed firm as we the children fanned out to other places. Dorchester was not supposed to be our destiny; we were meant, we thought, for better things. Even as those things became smaller, more realistic, more acceptable. We were in middle age now, and finding our way to the compromises we had abhorred in our own parents.

There was a decent showing for an old man who had retired a decade earlier and spent most of the intervening years in favored coffee shops, doing crossword puzzles and speaking out, Cassandra-like, about the ills of aluminum siding.

At the cemetery, some older men showed up, men I had never seen before. One of them laid across the flag-draped casket a small purple sash that had, embroidered, USS INDIANAPOLIS.

⁓

I was living in Virginia, outside DC, married to a woman I'd met when I'd finally gone off to college, after saving up for two years working for a moving company, the owner a friend of my father's. More than a few years overdue after dropping out then figuring out what a mistake that had been. Our daughters were young, and they played with my brother and sisters' kids as the adults sat and remembered. After we had come back from the cemetery, we went to the attic.

Up there was the trunk that had never been opened, the key long lost. With my mother's permission, I forced the hinges open with one of my father's paint scrapers and then cut through with a hacksaw. Inside was all of it, but none: sailor uniforms, in both white and dark, with the three stripes of the ordinary seaman; discharge papers, shined shoes, and a couple of medals. I didn't recognize them. I did some prowling on the internet, and the first one made sense: Good Conduct. The second was more mysterious: Combat.

"Why didn't you tell me about this?" I said to my mother.

"When he got home, he said not to ask. He was so very young."

I shook my head, mystified.

He had spent the rest of his life talking, but not ever about that.

It didn't take long to sell the house. A young black couple with kids, to complement the young white family who'd bought the Waterses' place. My mother chose to take an apartment in Dorchester, to our surprise. "Too late for suburbs now," she said. "I know what I know."

She had found her work, and it made her happy in the end. She spent twenty-five years with the bank. She'd spent her own time on the switchboards, and then to other duties when switchboards disappeared, and with her pension and her savings, my parents in their retirement had not been left wanting. But the house now had to be emptied, with its layers of history piled in the basement: Besides the usual stored items that never came back out of storage, there were many dozens of paint cans and equipment, dried out with the years.

My daughters explored the house one last time as the movers took away the furniture. My younger one had a flashlight and she went to the little door in the wall next to my third-floor bedroom. The laundry chute. She beamed the light down, curious, and said, "There's something there."

I took the flashlight, stuck my head in the chute, and looked.

There they were: my green bell-bottoms, caught on a wept nail, hanging there after thirty-two years.

I took a broom and poked the handle around until the pants fell. They were furred with the dust of all those years, and outside I beat them against a tree. I showed my mother and she said, "I don't remember those."

When we got back home, I took the bell-bottoms into the bathroom and pulled them on. They were tight, but with some effort I got the zipper to enclose me. The must of decades rose up from them. They were three inches too short for my legs now.

When I came from the bathroom, my daughters howled with delight. The foolish choices we had all made; the Kodachrome oversaturation of what that time had been. My wife, in the spirit, went to the stereo and found the station that played all the songs from those days. What came on was "Play That Funky Music, White Boy." What a great song!

I began to dance, and while the women in my life shrieked, I was doing it not to amuse them but to find my way back. The way we'd danced was ridiculous, but the way people danced now was equally so. Not that much really changes.

So I danced, at least, like the fool I had been in 1968, when nothing was a given, when I'd fallen and gotten up so many times, and when we had all been trying to find any of the right answers at all.

PART THREE

The Big Impossible

1

Migration, 1959

I was trying to get to higher ground. On the side of the road, I stood squinting into the far-off and setting sun. The distant sawtooth of peaks quivered at the hem of steely blue sky. I believed I could distinguish the taste of this thinning air from that of lower places. This bright air, cleaner than what I'd moved through and sweated in these last few years. Behind me, far down that road, the eastern horizon was as straight as a table; impossibly ahead of me was the knife's serration.

The night's cold would be enough that you could die. On the high plains, and getting dark fast. I'd been dropped here two hours before by a pickup truck that had turned north up long dirt roads. The sun had still felt strong. I fixed my stare on the forsaken end of the world and waited until something crested it, a speck of truck, twin pinpricks of light, as surprising as undiscovered stars. Something coming up on me, maybe my prayed-for lift.

⌒

I'd thrown everything away except the cash into the Platte River, at Grand Island, Nebraska. All the days I'd traveled, that wallet had stayed a lump of recollection I could not abide. A driver's license, yellowed receipts, faded pictures I didn't want to look at anymore. Unbearable weight. I'd long since become excommunicated from what I'd once lived.

I'd stood at that meager water, the crossing to a new shore. The Platte's banks were alluvial steppes indicating other incarnations, possibilities to swell and flow. I moved out to the center of the span, dead reckoning over that thin trickle. The wallet leather was shined over from years of sweat and friction. I would have been flattering myself if I thought people would be coming after me. I threw the wallet. It spun down, hit the low water, and floated. Then, as water steeped it, the wallet sank. All my papers. None would do me a bit of good anymore. I was long gone; I had far to go.

⌒

I stood in the bathroom of a Phillips 66 truck stop off Highway 40. The bathroom had the same colors as the gleaming outside sign—red, white, black—which hung over the road like a low moon. I looked in a veined mirror and sized it all up: rough-cut hair, windburned red face, the T-shirt and the grimy jeans and beaten leather jacket. I wasn't young, but I wasn't too old to not think I could still change. That mattered: that point in your life where the old part is dead and fallen away, and the new part isn't anything yet. You just are. You look in that cracked glass and see a face that can't quite start all over, can't erase the invested years, can't bargain for many more. Maybe you're just priming a bad ending. You stand in an unheated bathroom of a Shell station

and in the pall of the light of three in the morning, and you have
no idea what comes next.

⌒

I went to find the driver. His truck, a brand-new and waxed 1957
Peterbilt with a radiator as tall as a cathedral. The truck growled
in the fogged-white glow under a high stanchion. Bits of snow
danced under the lamplight in jolting trajectories, tracing like
moths. The driver wasn't around. He'd picked me up just before
dark and we'd listened to his cowboy music on the radio and
ridden miles without speaking, without any sense of friendliness.
Now we had stopped here. He knew people, at this stop. He'd
gotten out and hitched his tooled belt up under his gut, and he
told me I should stay away from the truckers' area.

"Just because I gave you a ride doesn't mean you're with me,"
he said. I guessed him to be pushing fifty, with a thick neck and
a face that couldn't seem to slough off its anger.

After an hour of waiting, I went to look. The truckers'
lounge was down a hall behind the counter in the store area.
The room was overly warm and looked like somebody's basement den. Dirty carpeting and nubby plaid chairs and a TV
with a washed-out picture. There were piles of skin magazines.
The truckers were mostly fat and mostly ugly. I looked around
and the driver, in one of the chairs, glanced my way. He rocked
forward and was on his feet, coming at me.

In the hallway, he said, "I told you to stay back."

⌒

Out in the parking lot, I followed him out to the truck. I stood at the edge of the light and he climbed in, grumbling. He said, "Just get in."

His arms still had some size, but were brown and wattled, as if the muscles had once filled the skin. His face was leathery along one side, after years of taking sun at the big steering wheel.

We started up and rolled onto the highway. The cab bucked when he levered into a new gear. He was hauling crates of machine bearings, and the truck struggled, even on near-level ground. He was going to Pueblo, which meant I was. I didn't have anyplace better to go. I'd kept the money from the wallet. It wasn't much. I'd rolled it up and put it in my underwear, snugged up. It was uncomfortable, but it made me know it was there.

The driver said, "What do you do when you get there?"

"Get a job," I said.

"What is it that you do?"

"I guess I'll try to figure that out when I get there."

He sniffed, annoyed. He drove silently.

⌒

We'd been driving a long time when the driver said, "You awake?"

"Yeah," I said.

"You got no money, right?"

"Right."

"So how about you take care of things now?" he said. "I'll pull over along here somewhere and you can pay the freight."

The dashboard lights barely lit him; I could see he was staring straight ahead.

"I mean it," he said.

"No," I said, shifting on the passenger seat. "I don't think so."

He let off a grunt. "Maybe you don't understand what I'm saying. That's the way it works on the road."

"Not interested," I said, slowly.

"I gave you a ride," he said.

"I already told you—not interested."

He didn't answer but shifted down and the weight of the truck's load put pressure on our backs, and then the shoulder of the road was crunching under the wheels. The truck took a long time to get stopped, and when it was still, he said, "Get out."

"Not interested in that, either," I said.

"Out," he said. It had been a long time since I had seen the lights of any town and the wind shrieked cold.

"No, to 'out,'" I said, so low it might have been a whisper. He might have had a gun, but I knew he was in a worse jackpot than I was.

"Get the truck on the road and drive," I said. I had nothing, and that was the only power I had now. An exhausted kind of fearlessness, not at all like bravery. For the first time now, I had made a decision that said I truly wanted to live.

He sat breathing through his nose. We were in close quarters, less than an arm apart, with the glass of the windows separating us from frigid expanses that seemed as much a void as airless space. The radio played on softly, some yodeling crooner going on about broken hearts. The engine pulsed beneath us. Many long minutes passed. Then he let up the clutch.

"I could kill you if I wanted," he said.

"You could try," I said. If he had a gun it would be to his left; he'd have to bring it all the way around. I'd be watching. There'd be no sleep and no quiet thoughts. His shoulders rose and tightened, ready. He put the truck into gear. We had three hours to go to Pueblo.

2

Grass Fire

I had come across a long job and pulled some money together and bought some clothing, and I had used more of it to get on toward Denver. I bought a leather jacket off a rack in a charity store, but it was in good shape, and that about finished off my earnings. I was sitting in a cafe in a small town using the last of my money on coffee when somebody came in and said there was a fire.

This was late afternoon, early spring. The clouds were heavy and the sky sparking with far-off hits of lightning. It seemed that half the men in that café were volunteer firefighters. Everyone went outside, onto the black asphalt apron of parking lot, to look at the horizon. The prairie grass was on fire just outside of town. Somebody's grazing land was burning away, and men were getting in their trucks, heading out, heading out to do something.

"Any of you others who want to help, can," one older man said. He looked at me with my pack and he said, "There might be a little bit of money in it."

I left my things in the café and rode out to the fire with that man, and he didn't ask me any questions. My general thought was to work at the fire, refuse payment for my effort, and ingratiate myself enough to get some further work and avoid the inevitable, whatever that would be.

The old man seemed to think the fire needed to be put out. I said I had heard that the fires could be a good thing, good to grow the grass back better, but the old man said, "Nobody's got the luxury to wait. The cattle need the grass now, not in a month or two. The question is if it's on your side of the property line that everything's burning up." I didn't know much about all that, so I didn't pursue it.

We got out to where the fire was burning. The flames were a jagged glowing line between green and black, the sheet of smoke gray and thin. The wind was gusting and the whole thing was moving toward the road like a burning string. Men were running along the line, some with shovels to turn dirt on the flames, others with burlap sacks to beat them out. The whole effort seemed like vaudeville. But this was a man's livelihood, so I kept my impressions to myself. I got out and the old man handed me a sack from the back of his truck and I ran around enthusiastically beating out flames until the fire, after a few hours and a dwindling wind, just seemed to lose its desire and burned itself out.

Our job done, more or less, we all rode back triumphantly. When we got there the café was locked, with my gear inside. Men got in their trucks and drove off. The sky was in twilight.

"You come with me," the old man said. "I can put you up until the morning. Then you can get your things."

It was getting cold and I had left my leather jacket at the café, along with my rucksack of meager clothing, and my money in a pocket of it. Stupidly. I had known going out of that place that I shouldn't have done it, but I had already gotten out to the parking lot when the old man had motioned me to his truck.

"Let me give you some money," he said now.

"Hey, no need. People seemed nice here. I was just happy to help out."

He grunted and I knew I was in, if just for a night or two. I was living my life in small cycles, the way a man crossing a tough river thinks only of the next rock to grab. Whatever money he would have given me was less than what I thought I could get this way. I didn't feel bad about this. If it was a few days' work, I'd earn my keep.

⌒

The old man had me inside his house for dinner. The meal reminded me of something I'd have seen in an old magazine—the peas and whipped potatoes and loose meat with gravy and bread and butter and glasses of milk. The man's wife sat quietly and smiled nervously at me when I caught her eye. I forced myself to eat slowly, as if I ate meals like this all the time.

"Where were you heading?" he said. His head was bowing over his plate and he slurped in some potatoes.

"Toward Oregon, eventually," I said. "I have family there." Neither was true. "They might help me get work. It's just going to take a while, I think."

He looked at me while he chewed his meat. I didn't have an accent and I think the inflection spoke of city, and of an origin different from what he was used to.

"What kind of work?" he said.

"Any work that pays enough," I said.

It was right then that I thought he'd offer something, but he didn't. He watched me take more helpings and glanced at his wife, who smiled on. A moment that had seemed imminent faded. The old man pushed himself away from the table and said, "You can stay in the shed."

He had a corrugated-steel outer building and we walked up there in the dark. He snapped on the light and that snap echoed around the beams. Inside that shed, it seemed colder than outside.

He went to a workbench and he gave me a ground cloth to wrap myself in. "I'd have you in the house but there really isn't a place and it would make the wife nervous," he said. I didn't have anything to say.

The canvas was stiff with the cold and I bent it around me. I was tired and I'd eaten my fill, but it was cold and my jacket was locked up in that café. I walked around the shed looking in the dark for a place to lie down, someplace protected. I burrowed under the workbench and found a bag of feed for my head. I wasn't going to sleep much, but there was no other choice.

⌒⌒

At dawn I dragged myself out from under the bench, my neck muscles leaden with the tensing against the cold. I was surprised that he wasn't up already, chores in the dark the way other farmers did. I was shivering and at times the shivering became convulsive; I saw his Chevy truck off by the shed and when I saw it was unlocked I got in. When I saw the keys in the ignition

I went ahead and started it up and put the heater on full roar. Those Chevys had good heaters and I only wanted to warm the cab up enough to stop shivering.

The old man was right out of the house, pulling his coat on as he hustled up. I opened the window of the truck and said "I just needed to warm up!"

He stood there, breathing heavy through his nostrils. He accused me of nothing, but neither did he seem to accept my explanation. "I'll get you into town now," he said. "Slide on over."

The café was crowded, as it had been the day before. I walked in with the old man and a few of the men already there stared outright. They watched me as I went to the corner of the place where I had left my things.

"They're not here," I said.

Nobody said anything. I went to the man at the counter and said, "My jacket and pack were there yesterday."

"I don't know anything about that," he said.

"Where's the owner?" I said.

He glared at me. "I am the owner," he said.

"I need to find my things," I said. My bag was useless to anybody else—the rolled clothes were barely worth keeping, except that I had nothing else. I had on my boots and jeans and my heavy shirt, but as the sun faded I knew I'd suffer from the cold. The money wouldn't have been much to anyone else.

The owner looked at the old man and the old man shrugged.

"I didn't see any things," the owner said.

"I don't believe this," I said.

"I ought to be going," the old man said. "I can drop you up the road."

A younger man sitting at the counter swiveled on his stool. "Say, Earl, I can do that for you," he said. "I'll take the man out to the road."

"Thanks, Chuck," Earl said. "That's a fine idea."

"Wait a minute. I need to find my things," I said. "I don't go up the road until then."

"You locked up the café when the fire started," I said to the owner. "I helped with the fire and then I came back and my things were locked up."

"I don't know anything about that," the owner said.

I motioned toward the old man. "Earl will tell you I helped at the fire."

Earl nodded. "That he did."

The owner said, "It wasn't here when I opened up."

Chuck didn't say anything driving. He was much bigger than I was and he kept his eye on me. He was taking me out to a crossroads where I was more likely to find a ride. I had no money and no coat and no extra clothing, and the clouds were coming in from the west.

We passed the charred expanses where the fire had burned that day before. Chuck looked at it with interest and seemed for a moment to forget I was there next to him.

At the crossroads he pulled over and looked at me. He waited for me to get out. I did, and I thought he might say something, but he didn't and I slammed the door shut.

I already had a plan in my mind, which was to go back. I could find my way to the old man's ranch and steal the truck. The keys would be there out of habit that couldn't be bent by one day's events. Or I could break into the café and take what was there—if not cash, then food. I would only take what I needed to get out of the position I'd been put in, trying to help. I was forming a way of thinking that said it was okay, that only sought to avoid the real chance of freezing on a roadside, hungry. I had been a man in a warm coat just trying to get up the road, but that had changed now.

I watched Chuck's pickup become a speck and then drop from the horizon. I could stand for a bit and maybe, with luck, a ride would show up and it would be all the way to Denver and there'd be a job to have and I'd find a way to get a new coat. I wondered how likely that kind of providence was.

The wind was strong and I walked a little down the road to get into a trough. The line where the fire had stopped was ahead. There didn't seem to be any reason it had halted just there, although there must have been some combination of elements that made that happen at this precise point, and even as I examined it there seemed to be no real reason to it. I stood straddling the line, the black waste of the fire to my left, the fertile green of pasture to my right.

3

The Big Impossible

T his motel was at the edge of Garden City, Kansas. It had two wing-like rows of rooms with the red doors facing a weed-grown blacktop apron. At the center was an A-frame lobby so that the whole thing had the cumbersome feel of a transport plane trying to will itself from a dusty airstrip. In the front of the lobby, across the parking lot, was a chain-link-fenced rectangle within which there was a small swimming pool. It fronted the place as if on display, and the part of the fence facing the road was slatted with green plastic strips. It was a place the last of my money could take me, for a night. A late-October Friday, Indian summer, warm. Kansas was not at as high an altitude as Colorado, and the air held its heat better.

I didn't have a swimsuit. I hadn't had short pants since I was a boy. My duffel held only necessary work clothes and personal effects. I stripped off my shirt and boots and socks and went to the pool in my filthy jeans. No one was within the fence and I only had the idea of letting my skin warm to a dusty breeze that had kicked up from the western horizon.

I had my eyes closed and didn't realize I was asleep until the sliding door of a van slammed shut and made me start. It emptied itself of a woman about my age and a half-dozen preteen girls who seemed to lumber toward the lobby door in a way that suggested a long and tiring ride. The woman looked at me a little warily. Whether it was my right to be there or not, I knew those girls were going to want to swim, and not with someone as shaky-looking as me around. I pulled myself from my chaise and went back to my room.

Television seemed like an odd indulgence. The black-and-white sat on a rickety cart next to the dresser. A man read the news and told me things I hadn't an inkling of. The smell of Garden City, the stockyards and packing plant, was strong but seemed pure in its earthy funk. I was hungry but was biding my time to make the whole night meal one to sustain me for a while. I could hear the little girls out in the water now, squealing and plunging, and when it was quiet I pulled a room chair out in front of my door to feel the cooling air of those high plains.

In the parking space that went with the room next to mine, a big Cadillac, new-looking, was nosed up at the walk like a moored ship. The car had California plates; it was powder blue with white leather seats. The trunk was still open, as was the door to the room, and after a while the man came out to get the rest of his things.

He was tiny. He was maybe a little more than three feet tall. I guessed him to be in his sixties and he turned and saw me standing there. In a reedy voice, he said, "Give an old fellow a hand?"

I got up and went around to the trunk and took out his bag, which was leather and expensive-looking. He had thick glasses and the eyes seemed a mile under them and his face was all lines. I brought the suitcase in and laid it at the foot of his bed; he slipped his hand in his pocket for just an instant, and then he said, "Say, let me offer you a drink. I'll join you outside."

He had already brought in a smaller leather case, and he opened it to reveal a red-velvet-lined compartment that held a bottle of Chivas, a metal jigger, and four glasses secured by small leather straps. He set up on top of the dresser, and sent me for ice. When I came back and he had trickled the Scotch over the ice, we went outside, him carrying the drinks with his palms underneath, me carrying his chair out to put next to mine.

"Where are you headed?" I asked.

"I have to be down in Liberal in the morning," he said. "You?"

"Looking for work," I said. "Indulging myself for one night." He, with his car and his leather luggage and his Scotch, was clearly slumming, in a dingy motel he hadn't wanted, but he nodded and said nothing.

After a while, he said, "Call me Frank."

A blue Air Force station wagon with a serial number stenciled on the driver's side door rolled into the lot. Four young men got out, in jumpsuits and colorful ascots. They were clean-cut and joking, relaxed with benign smiles. Frank and I watched them take out their bags and go to the office.

"Jet pilots, they must be," Frank said.

We sat and finished our drinks and he fixed us a couple more. After a while the woman and the little girls came out to the van, their hair still slick from the pool. The woman, having forgotten something, fumbled with her keys and went back in

192 / EDWARD J. DELANEY

the room. One by one, the girls saw the little man and one of them said something nasty and the others tried, not overly hard, to suppress their giggles.

"A lifetime of that," Frank said, clearly to put me at ease. "Living like you're comfortable with what life deals you, that's the big impossible sometimes."

The little girls couldn't stop staring. Another remark, and another louder round of squeals. The woman came out, got in the van, and they drove off.

"What business are you in?" I said.

"I'm pretty much retired," Frank said.

"You're traveling for fun?"

"No," he said. I could tell he didn't especially care to get into it. "Every once in a while, my services are in demand. It's a way of making a little money quickly and easily. Then I can go home."

"Where do you live?" I said.

"Rancho Mirage, California."

"You drove all that way?"

"I drive everywhere. I won't fly. Can't stand the thought."

"Flying is safer."

"Don't even try," he said.

Two of the Air Force men came out of the rooms in swim trunks with towels over their shoulders. They had shower sandals on and they were heading for the pool. Frank sat tilting his drink back and forth, watching. "But I always wanted to learn to fly," he said.

He was lost in himself for a second, then he turned to me. "I notice you have no vehicle. What is it that you do?"

"I work," I said. "I have to get to places where the jobs are. I just finished on a farm out east of here. I'm walking into town tomorrow to get a bus."

"Good work, hard work," he said.

"Yes," I said.

"That's good."

The fliers seemed to swim without enjoyment. Each of them went in, floated and then put his head under, then came up and toweled off. They snapped their metal watches back on their wrists and came back across the parking lot.

"So you boys are pilots," Frank called out. The two looked at each other then veered toward us.

"We're with SAC, sir," one of them said softly.

"What kinds of planes do you fly?" Frank said.

"We don't fly, sir. We're launch officers."

Frank looked at me.

"They mind the missiles," I said. I had been on those farms where the silos lay flat and fenced like tombs, to be worked around, both on combines and in conversation. These men went down holes where they waited for orders that weren't ever supposed to come.

One of the men gave off the snort of a laugh. "We mind them, yes, sir."

They walked off toward their room. Frank watched.

"They sit underground," I said. "If somebody sends the right code, they push the buttons."

"From their uniforms you'd think they were fliers," Frank said.

For a few moments I thought about robbing Frank. In my

situation at that time, the thought was almost inevitable whenever I met someone new: the car, gassed up with the keys
nearby; his wallet inevitably fat; me, both visible and invisible,
the name on the register not mine, and the room paid in cash.
But I thought about him without his car. Flying out of that little Garden City airport, strapped into an eggbeater. Frank was
my friend.

A door opened down the way and two of the girls came out,
barefoot, heading toward the ice machine in the lobby with their
square plastic bucket. As they approached us they squeezed
together and speeded up and as they got ten feet past us burst
into giggles.

Frank didn't say anything. He took a long swig from his
drink. The girls were down the way now, sitting on the edge of
the cement. One of them would say something, and the others
would act as if they were trying not to laugh, which made them
laugh more. Every once in a while I'd glance over and see them
looking, and they'd look away.

"You can see I've done nothing to bring that on," Frank said,
staring ahead.

"Who knows what they're up to," I said. I was used to being
invisible.

"Yes, there is a possibility that they're laughing at you,"
Frank said dryly, and then he got up to make us more drinks.

Near dusk, two of the missile men came out with a baseball
and mitts and began to play catch in the open area between the
motel and the pool. They started with some easy throws and
then began to lob the ball higher, firing it up into the fading blue

sky until they were fully exerting themselves, trying to outdo each other. At the crest of its arc the ball seemed to silver, neither rising nor falling; it hung lighted in the sun against deep blue; the sense of it falling back was only something to be sensed gradually. When the ball fell into a mitt, the pop of it rattled around against the flat boards of the building. They must have been good when they were younger. They threw and caught with a loose easiness. At one point Frank said, "Neither one of them has dropped it yet." But the day was about over. The sun fell; the colors went dead. The ball now became a black dot straining against gray sky. They played until the yellow bug lights went on along the breezeway.

I was thinking about the softness of the bed, the dry touch of clean sheets. But Frank wanted to talk and he was making the drinks so I stayed in the chair, next to him.

"I've done a million jobs, all pretty well," Frank said. "But I never found the one that did it for me. I can appreciate the fact you're looking for something."

"It's more out of necessity," I said.

"Bullshit," he said. "Big guy, young enough, sounds like he has half a brain. You've made choices that I'm not going to ask you about."

"I appreciate that, Frank."

There came that point when Frank's head began to sag and I knew he'd need to go to bed. He was as small as a child and I could have carried him easily, but it seemed demeaning, to both of us. This man was a gentleman and so I was trying to be. His money would have been easy to take, but I didn't want to be a thief. I wanted to be a man, like him, with a car and a wallet and a home to go back to. It was envy of a general kind, and it should not have been that hard to find simple things.

"Frank, go to bed," I said loudly. The head came up and he grunted and pulled himself to his feet. He stared at me and I knew I was lost to him now. He shuffled into the room and slammed the door shut.

I still had his glass in my hand. When I was finished, I put it on the hood of his car, where he'd see it. When I got in bed I thought I'd be asleep in a minute, but the bed felt too soft. I couldn't get used to it, and somewhere in the night I spread the blanket on the floor and slept until dawn.

In the morning I dressed and walked down the road to a store where I could get a razor. The sun was just up and the Air Force car was already gone. Back toward the motel I saw the little girls coming out of their room. They were identically dressed. Blue-checked dresses and white blouses underneath and ankle socks and glittering red shoes. Pigtails. Red lipstick. As I got closer I must have looked confused because when the woman came out, and saw me looking, she said, "They're all Dorothy."

"Yes, I see," I said. "Why?"

The Oz Festival is down in Liberal today," she said. "There's a look-alike contest. We came all the way from North Dakota."

"I didn't know they did those kinds of things."

"You didn't know you were sitting with a real Munchkin?" she said.

I knew who Frank was then. I thought of him sleeping hard in his bed, with his outfit laid out.

Inside I undressed and shaved and then used the razor to

THE BIG IMPOSSIBLE / 197

hack away at my hair. I threw the clumps in the toilet until the water was skinned with hair and then I flushed it all down. I turned on the shower and felt it become nearly scalding then I stepped in.

My bus didn't leave town until noon, so I had some time. I stepped out of the shower and turned on the television and stood watching it with my towel wrapped around me. I heard the reverberation of a door opened, and through the slight parting of the curtains I could see Frank struggling his bag into the car. He had on knee britches and striped stockings and shoes with curling toes, and a tight-fitting waistcoat. My mind went back to those long-ago images on a screen, of those tiny people. Frank saw the glass on the hood. He took it, opened the car door, and tossed the glass on the leather seat. Pulling out of the parking lot, he pushed the gas a little too hard, kicking out a cloud of gravel and dust.

Buried Men

I had heard the stories the whole time, about some ranch of indeterminate location, of indeterminate distance from here, where the men were buried. There was a place out there, somewhere on the dark borderlands, where evil resided. That year I had fallen in with an itinerant group of custom cutters and some others who were pickers, working our way north from Oklahoma as the harvest fell later in each successive latitude. I can't remember who mentioned it first, but on a long ride somewhere the talk came around to a place where men, without last names and without histories, disappeared.

I was skeptical. I rode in backs of trucks and I listened to these stories and wondered where they came from, wondered what kind of vague intimidation they represented. I supposed it was a way that our employers—family men with safes in their houses and guns under their beds—kept us in line, the nameless, hungry, vaguely hostile men they hired to work their fields.

We were riding out to the work on a flatbed when a guy who I'd seen around began to get into it. He had the itch, the shaking and scratching that I sometimes saw in guys who were starting to fall apart, and he couldn't stop the yammering over the grinding engine.

"What about the one named Bobby Something?" he shouted as we banged over the ruts. "First he's around, then he was gone. I mean, what the hell happened to him?"

"What?" somebody said.

"Everybody says there's this ranch where you work for the guy, then he kills you and buries you out somewhere. He or *them*. I don't know how many are in on it."

"*What?*"

"What or why? I dunno! To kill a guy? Sick bastard? To work a guy like a slave and then not have to pay him?"

"Where is this ranch?" I said, just so it was as if anyone was really listening.

"Somewhere over in east Colorado," he said with a finality that bespoke knowledge.

In those days I tended not to say much, but this time I did.

"Oh, bull*shit*," I said. "Where do you hear this?"

He looked wounded by my attack. I had found that for the most part these itinerant workers were gentle, broken-down men, and that they didn't want trouble. I was sure he had gotten into it just to pass the moment, to fill dead air, but for whatever reason I couldn't let it go now.

"It's true," he said. "I knew the guys."

"You don't know the guys," I said. "You don't even know his name. *Bobby Something.* You can't know what happened to him. He just went somewhere else."

"If he went somewhere else, I would have heard about it."

"How? How? Who knows where I am right now, except you guys on this truck? I get off this truck, I'm gone."

"No," he said. "Doesn't happen that way. We know you. The Tall Guy. The one who used to work with us. The one with the leather jacket. The guy with the hand," he said. "The one everybody noticed 'cause he sure as hell didn't fit this picture. Six months from now, somebody says, 'What happened to the tall guy with the leather jacket? The guy with the burns on his hand? Somebody else says, 'I seen him in Tulsa,' or whatever. If nobody's heard anything, we know something happened."

"That can't be possible," I said. "None of us even knows who we are." They all had been taking it in, and now they exchanged looks, memorizing.

"When you hear that nobody's heard about a guy, it makes you wonder."

"I don't know any of you," I said.

"You know us whether you want to or not."

"Who's missing?" I said. "Name one of them."

"I can't remember the names. There was that guy with the beard. He was kind of fat. And the Mexican guy with the tattoo that said SATAN LIVES."

"I never saw him," I said. I watched the slow slide of the horizon and thought about dried-up trails and lost ties that made people unmissable.

Over the next six months, as I worked my way slowly toward the northwest, working fields with men like myself, men who didn't care to give much away, I heard those stories. Disappeared men. Men shot in the backs of their heads while they drank water; men hit in their sleep with foot-long crescent wrenches. Dragged and buried, dirt turned over them as they bled cold.

Everybody knew the exact details, but none of the details ever matched up. Everybody knew the men killed, but no one could place a name. The ranch was somewhere in Colorado, somewhere in Wyoming, somewhere in west Kansas.

I saw the little guy from the truck, trying to find winter work in Denver. I had been living in the basement of a rectory, and I'd had to leave. Work was scarce and I'd gone to a day-labor office trying to find city work. I saw him and when he saw me he said, "Yeah." He had seemed to have developed even more tics; the nose jumped as if he were about to sneeze. He reminded me of a sniffing dog.

While we waited, we stood in line together. "I heard you were laying low," he said.

I shook my head and grinned. "What does that even mean?" I said. "That could mean anything. That means nothing."

I had learned that in these circles names were not asked for, only offered, and I did neither. But he went ahead of me to fill out his work card, and I saw his name was Ray.

When he turned he saw me looking over his shoulder. He grinned. I signed my card using a name that wasn't mine. His name might not have even been Ray. Nobody was required to prove it.

We sat in the waiting area of the day-labor office. It had rows of molded-plastic seats like a bus station. We waited silently through the morning to be called. They called by the numbers on our cards, and my number didn't come up, nor did Ray's. In those day-labor places you were glad for a warm place where you more or less belonged, but as the day wore on, if your number wasn't called, you'd start thinking about where you'd get any food and if you'd be sleeping under a bridge. I looked through the window and watched bare trees sway against gray skies and knew I should just feel the warmth while it was there. But knowing that the warmth came with the promise of a colder night made me nearly resent it.

Ray was having no better luck than I was. We all wanted indoor work.

"They got the heat too high in here," Ray said, even though he kept his jacket on.

"Yeah," I said.

"I seen that guy before, the one who went out about an hour ago. With the Army jacket. I seen him in Bismarck about two years ago."

"What's his name, Ray?"

"I don't know. What's yours?"

I didn't answer.

"You shy, or on the run?" he said.

"You don't need to know that," I said.

⌒

I was sleeping in someone's barn, wrapped in a handed-out bed-roll from the man who had employed me at that moment. I was dreaming, which was unusual, for my sleep was usually blank and heavy. It wasn't a dream, really, just a memory, coming to me from where forgotten things hide.

In the dream there were hands on me. I understood in the dark of it that these were my father's hands, taking me out of the back seat of a car. Some drive, from somewhere, at night. I could remember those drives. The long network of family, my father driving through night to touch those distant nodes, darkness around him like the shrouding clothes of a desert traveler, the eyes the only thing seen, in the square rectangle of light that shone off the rearview. All, lost. The hands took me and I was carried, through a door, up some stairs. His arms held me as if I were weightless, a familiar burden. He was long gone, but I still felt his grip. Up stairs and toward something. The sensation was like rising through water to some light and air.

I awakened, shivering. I was in a dark barn in the middle of a vast prairie. All around me were broken-down men, dreaming their own dreams of memory, because none of us allowed ourselves anything beyond the work we would rise to do tomorrow. I wondered if I had made any noises.

The work was rote and if you could grind away at it you could find a way to make it mindless, working the hands through dirt and roots to pull at something and throw it in a basket, to climb through a tree snapping the fruit from its branches; the best thing was to live in the small cycles of each reach of the hand, each small piece gathered.

We went to the house for lunch, where it was laid out on long tables under the trees. There were a dozen men working and we ate fast and slyly, the act of getting one's fair share, however one estimated that. No talking, only the spooning of food and the filling of a hunger that was as real as a limb.

My hair was almost always long, because I had nothing to cut it with. In hard rains I'd wring and rub it and scrape out bugs with my fingernails, which I kept short by grinding them down against pavement, sitting on the lip of a road, waiting low for a vehicle to crest the edge of land.

When I saw a pay phone, at a truck stop or out in front of a small-town restaurant, I thought of numbers still glued in my head, how I could have dialed those numbers and made myself a pulsing voice from a void, if there was any point.

I got a job pulling carrots in a field in New Mexico. I was heading south as the fall approached. There were days without eating, and lightheaded returns to the fields, working on nothing for enough to restore what was lost, a no-win game.

Out here they had called it the "carrot capitol of the United States," but in 1950 a Navajo shepherd named Paddy Martinez had discovered uranium up on Haystack Mesa. Most of the men worked the mines, and farmers had to bring in people like us to do the work. "Lot of money in those mines," Ray said, again and again. "We're not good enough for that work. Only family men get to touch that uranium." In time, I went off by myself just to get away from Ray and his endless talk.

The farmer we were working for was a heavy-shouldered, middle-aged, and probably with some Spanish in him. He acted as his own foreman, and, as we bent over with our burlap sacks, he kicked clods of dirt and loomed up at our flanks. Working, I watched his shadow crawl up behind me. I'd have been a fool not to watch my back, but Ray's constant jabbering about disappearing men had me watching all the more.

I stood up straight and turned at him.

"Tired of working already?" he said.

"No, I just thought you needed something."

"I don't. So work."

I went down to a knee and listened for him to move, which he didn't. I was far off from the others, but I knew I was in the open. What could he do?

In the setting sun we sat to meager portions of food the farmer laid out after the day in the fields. We had all looked at one another disgustedly and ate down what was there. The idea of eating pulled carrots crusted in dirt had no appeal; in the apple trees we worked far north you could eat, hidden in the boughs on the ladder. Whether this farmer was cheap or broke didn't matter: You didn't short your workers on their meal without some trouble from it.

In the evening, after we had eaten, I wandered off toward the irrigation ditches, trying to find a quiet place. The mosquitoes were bad down in that valley, and if you had the money you would smoke a cigar to ward them off. I slapped at them and moved toward drier sections where the clouds of them, flitting jaggedly, dissipated.

I had a chocolate bar. I had taken it off the counter in the kitchen of the house, after we had eaten out in the yard. I had only gone to the screen door to ask for water, but no one had been there. The chocolate bar was put out, and close, and I reached in without ever setting a foot inside. It wasn't a sin to take food from a man who was starving you.

Down along the dry ditch, I sat on the berm and ate the chocolate. It was molded into big square blocks and I snapped each of them off between my teeth, then rolling them in my mouth until the squares rounded themselves and I had fashioned chocolate balls. I felt some pulse coming back into me. It began to seep into my mind that this was the first time since I was a child that I had actually stolen something.

When I was finished, I crumpled the foil and threw it into the ditch. I got up and wiped my hands on my filthy pants and walked back through the near-darkness toward the house.

I saw someone coming, and it took me getting up to a half-dozen yards to see it was the farmer. In the near-dark I couldn't see an expression but when he said,"Where were you?" the tone told me that man was highly pissed off.

"Walking," I said.

"To where?"

"Just walking," I said.

"You didn't get enough exercise working today?" he said.

"I guess not."

I thought right then he was going to accuse me of something, but he didn't. He walked by me and began walking down where I had come from.

Somebody had started a fire to keep the bugs off us. I sat close to the smoke and didn't particularly think of anything. I waited until I felt I could sleep. I got up, arched my back, and began to walk toward the barn. The farmer had been waiting, I think; he'd been sitting on his concrete steps smoking a cigarette, and from an angle I saw him coming toward me.

"My daughter had a chocolate bar from her grandma and now it's gone," he said.

"I don't know anything about that."

"Fuckin thieves working for me," he said. "My daughter crying about it."

"That's too bad," I said.

"You ever hear of a place where they shoot guys like that? In in the back of the head?" he said.

"I never once heard of that," I said.

"They bury them and nobody ever knows—"

"And where would this place be?" I said.

"Maybe you'll find out, smart guy," he said.

I knew the moment he said it there was no such place, that there never was, that it was built on the bullshit of a hundred guys like this one. I took a goddamn candy bar!

"Oh," I said. "Is *this* the place?"

"Maybe it is."

I spat and shook my head. "So show me that last guy who got shot in the back of the head over a candy bar."

"Nobody would ever know he was gone," he said. "You're nobody."

Of course he was siding in the argument I'd made all along.

"It wouldn't be that easy," I said.

"You got a wise mouth," he said. "You get your things and you get out."

"You ever hear of a place where guys who get screwed over come back and strangle the bastard. Nobody would ever know who it was. How do you catch nobody?"

"I never heard of that place," the farmer said. "So get the fuck out."

So now I was shit out of a job.

"Pay me what you owe me," I said.

"I don't owe squat to a guy who threatens me," he said. "Get out before I get somebody down here." He went into his pocket and brought up a crumpled foil in his hand and he threw it on the ground at my feet.

Sleeping out beyond the carrot fields, I thought about what kind of people that people like me moved toward being. I tried to sleep with mosquitoes crawling into my ears, plotting a revenge as imaginary as the people who would have done me in.

Medicine

S he hears the sound through the window, a slamming of horse against wood in the stable. And then the silence, that endless three or four seconds when you convince yourself that all is well, and then the shriek of pain that confirms you've only fooled yourself. Peg drops the dish she's been drying, and as it shatters on the floor she's already shoving open the screen door, running. The barn, down the path, is really an outsized shed that keeps the old horse out of the weather. The screams radiate through the wallboards as Peg swings open the latch door and tries to see into the dark.

Bitsy is in the straw, her entire face covered in blood. She is four years old, the youngest grandchild. She is the most endearing and the most reckless of all the brood. Bitsy screams with the vigor that says she'll live, but that's all I'm sure about. The horse is edged guiltily up against the wall, its head lowered, its glance sidewise. My eyes adjust to the light: Bitsy has a gouge in her temple that looks an inch deep. Her hands shake as if peeled down to pure unthinking reflex. Her screams fill the barn like shining light.

"Call a damned doctor!" Peg wails.

Bitsy came to us when her mother couldn't square the childrear-
ing with the nights in the bars with the beer-can cowboys. Even in
our gathering old age, we were better to do this. I say "we." I am
the odd fit here, the boyfriend of the grandmother. I am a graying
man with a limping shuffle, but Bitsy has become my substance.

I run, struggling, back into the house. I pick up the phone and
when I speak I am almost crying. Peg stumbles up the walk, Bitsy
in her arms, the blood all over everything. Peg is wide-eyed with
fear, and rage, and sorrow. She looks at me and bares her teeth.

"Why weren't you watching her!" she screams.

The drive goes on and on. The hospital is four towns away. Peg
is in the back seat with Bitsy across her lap. Peg rages on while
Bitsy thrashes and forever bleeds, still crying wildly, the skin
going white, and then gray, under the gelatinous purple sheen
of the coagulating blood. My hands feel numb on the steering
wheel, and only once do I look through the rearview and meet
Peg's eyes, which come down on me hard and tell me what I am.

The deliverance is a matter of seconds. The hospital is a
squat cinder-block building off the main drag. Through the
swinging doors, rushing and shouting, Bitsy dumped on a gur-
ney and then swept away, nurses chasing. Then the gaunt and
sad-eyed GP, stethoscope hung around his neck like a stole,
noiselessly trailing. The waiting room is just a bend in a hallway
with some flat vinyl benches; the silence feels foreign and omi-
nous and we just stand there. Then Peg sits, and then I, shadowy
and uncertain, sit on the opposite edge of that long bench. She

will not look at me. The hours and days and years stretch ahead, as they had once stretched behind.

⌒

I remember a day: I was searching. I was driving the old pickup, which lurched and spat in its smoky death struggle. The engine had needed overhauling for a year, and it would never happen, and in that way it reminded me of myself, banged up but still game. I was searching for Dorothy. Bitsy was two and a half then, staying with us, and after nearly two weeks Dorothy had not come back to get her. We just wanted to know what was going on. We just wanted to confirm the obvious.

It had been Wednesday the third when Dorothy dropped off Bitsy. Now it was Thursday the eighteenth. Peg had stayed home with the child while I'd made the ambling drive, the customary search, watching the sun die off at the edge of the plains and go cold. We didn't want to change things, we just wanted to be sure Dorothy was in one piece. And we wanted the nod that said the deal was done. After two days we had known Bitsy wouldn't go back. After four days we'd heard from a friend of Peg's that Dorothy was making a commotion in the bar down off the yards, and didn't seem to have a worry in the world. Drunk or no, looking me in the eye or no—just a nod. That was all I needed to get. Dorothy was always a bad girl, the way I heard it. Dorothy was always a handful. We didn't want to challenge her into taking Bitsy back from us.

I'd been four places, the usual haunts, no luck. Dorothy tended to roam. When I'd left the house, the soft heat of the day beginning to let off, Bitsy was bathed and in her pajamas and on Peg's lap, as Peg watched *Laverne & Shirley*. Now, bouncing over some rutted side roads, I wanted to be there, too.

The bar I was looking for was one I'd heard about from the drivers down at the co-op—the kind of place that drivers at the co-op laughed about but didn't actually go near. It was rough in the way that married men with little houses imagine themselves in it, but to me it was familiar territory, whether I'd been there or not. The bar was over in a town called Midway, and didn't have a sign. I'd know it by the trucks, was my guess.

Other than missing Bitsy and Peg and our Thursday-night ritual, I didn't mind this part: the driving. The movement. My life had been the constant shift between two states of being: moving and wanting to be still, and being still and wanting movement. Aging was keeping me more still. Driving toward a tight cluster of lights down across the valley floor, I thought of the old urge for migration, and whether I couldn't fully shake its pull. There had been times when, gunning the truck out of town, that I have felt that familiar nausea.

Dorothy had an itch of her own. As best I could tell, her urge was for foamy beer and burning shots of bad liquor and a warm, stinking body next to her when she regained consciousness under dirty, twisted sheets. Bitsy, to hear Dorothy tell it, was an immaculate conception—she woke up that morning without even a trace of a man left behind, and she didn't bother trying to solve the riddle. Whatever man was handy seemed good enough, and that spread her over the better part of four counties.

Bitsy didn't come to us in a way that made Peg think she'd be a born-again parent. Dorothy had gotten comfortable dropping her off for us to mind, longer stretches each time; one day she showed up saying she was "checking in on her." I stood on the porch looking at the truck down the street, its slumping driver, its muddy anonymity. I heard Dorothy and Peg arguing, the tone hushed enough I couldn't make out the words, but heated enough I knew exactly what was being said. Then Dorothy came stamping out and the screen door slammed and then she was piling herself into the truck, gone.

I walked back in and Peg had the look of grief that is particular to people with doomed children. Bitsy was on the floor playing with some plastic rings.

"There's just no talking to that girl," Peg mumbled.

⌒

Now, here in the hospital, Peg looks over at me. The stress and the fluorescent lights don't flatter her, and her anger at me binds it all into a new face: This is the first moment I truly see her as an old lady.

"She better not die," Peg says to me in a voice so steady it's poison.

"Bitsy isn't gonna die," I say, as if I have any idea.

"She better not," Peg says, and goes looking in her bag for a cigarette.

⌒

Midway was just over a barbed-wired rise, the town a gully of a place with flat roofs and scrawny trees and carcasses of cars haunting the yards. I took it down to thirty per, and coasted through until I saw a long windowless wooden building with pickups nosed up to it like sucklings. I don't know what Dorothy was traveling in those days, but this place looked the part. I got out of the truck and chocked the wheels with rocks just to be sure.

I entered the place slowly, just another coot with a country thirst, staying down by the old cigarette machine near the door. Nobody bothered to look. I saw Dorothy instantly, hung over a butt and a tumbler down on the part where the bar curved toward the Gents. A high-traffic location, facing toward the swing door where many a man would emerge lightened and refreshed, again thirsting for what might be had. It was her way.

I came shuffling down, easy, trying not to spook her. When she caught me in the edge of things, she looked at the end of her cigarette like she was talking to it and said, "Well, look all what the cat drugged in." She had the subdued, heavy air of someone carrying a lot of alcohol but used to the load. Up close, the halo of her breath was ratty with the liquor and the smokes, her eyes glazed in a way that might have been mistaken for indifference, rather than the inability to meet the obvious emotion: Dorothy didn't like me, and never had; I'd come along and filled Peg's need not to pass her days in lonely silence, or in war with her daughter. I showed up, and Dorothy began to see that the ranting, screaming, and mental torture weren't going to be as welcome as they once had been.

I stood there, making sure not to appear angry.

"Your mama just wanted to make sure you were in one piece," I said.

"Well, here I am," she said, her voice lofting and then burning out like dud fireworks. It came out only as a statement, not nearly the anger she'd been trying to heave my way.

Consent is a funny thing. In a way, that was good enough to tell me what I needed to hear, but I went another step. I wasn't going to rush it, though. The bartender came floating down, solicitous, and I said, "What's coldest is best."

"Oh, hell," Dorothy said, knowing she had gotten some company now.

After an hour, Peg says, "It's been two hours!"

"Bitsy must be taking some pretty good stitches," I say.

"Her beautiful face!" Peg cries out, and the shoulders are heaving with the grief. "Her perfect little face!"

I sit listening to her cry. Peg is fifty and a grandma six times over. Her two good girls are married to farm boys out in the eastern end of the state; Peg, in their eyes, is shaded over by Dorothy's end of the equation, and now with live-in man—me— who hasn't got much to say about where he came from. Peg visits those grandkids without me at her side. I don't argue it. I spend those hours with Bitsy, watching her figure out the world from the middle of the outspiraling hooked rug.

Dorothy was down to the last cigarette in the pack, and she looked as if she was trying to hold off on it. Then she sighed and tapped it out and lit it up, still looking into her drink, still angled away from me.

"Well you can tell my mama you found me in one piece," she said. "That's what you needed, right?"

"Pretty much," I said.

"Okay, then," she said.

That was it, the nod I was looking for, but now I couldn't let this one go.

"Don't worry," I said. "Bitsy's *fine*."

She took this one like a slap, and whatever satisfaction I had from getting a reaction faded into the realization that I'd just picked a fight I didn't need to.

"What all is that supposed to mean?" Dorothy said.

"It means what it means," I said. "She's fine. She's in good hands, and you needn't worry."

Dorothy just stared me down.

"I'm a loving mother," she said.

I couldn't give her that one, even though I knew where it would all go now.

"I was letting you all have some time with her!" Dorothy shouted. "You don't appreciate that?"

I just stared at her. This was not what I was sent to do.

"I'll be there in the morning," Dorothy said, and she nodded for another drink for herself. "Have her ready for me to take her."

Peg, sitting down at the end of the bench in the waiting area, finally says,"How long could it take to find out what's going on?"

"I'm sure they're taking good care," I say.

We sit looking at the checkerboard tiles. When someone appears in the hallway, we look up expectantly, then drop our gazes when it turns out not to be who we're waiting for.

Peg sits looking at her hands and then lets off a long sigh.

"Well, I'm getting coffee. You want me to bring you some coffee?" Peg says.

"Yeah."

She gets up and straightens her clothes. She has pressed jeans on, and her cream-colored lady's boots, and a long blue blouse that was always her favorite. The blood on it has dried into something that almost looks like it's part of the fabric. Peg pats my shoulder and goes looking for a machine.

⌒

Dorothy showed up better than two days later, pulling herself unsteadily out of a rattling old El Camino. The driver didn't turn his head toward the house to see what was going on—it was clear he was just a ride, and a reluctant one at that.

"Well I'm here then," Dorothy yelled hoarsely through the screen door. I came through from the kitchen, looking at the time. It was past one in the afternoon, but Dorothy had the almond eyes that spoke of hangover and fragments of thoughts.

"Bitsy's not here," I said evenly.

"Well, where the damned hell is she?" Dorothy says.

"Your mama took her out for air," I say.

"I said I was coming to get her!"

"You said you were coming Friday morning. Today is not Friday. Today is Sunday afternoon. Your mama took Bitsy out while she went on her errands. Bitsy was ready Friday, like you wanted."

Dorothy's eyes fluttered with agitation and dilemma. But I saw it now, the half-heartedness of it. "Well," she said, "what am I supposed to do now?"

I looked at her blankly, a man with absolutely no ideas. She looked back at the El Camino. The man sat slumped behind the wheel, smoking.

"Well we can't sit around waiting forever," Dorothy said.

My hand moved around to my back pocket, and I brought the wallet out slowly. I looked through it and found a faded twenty.

"Here's something for his gas and lunch," I said. "So your friend won't be troubled by the effort."

Dorothy snapped the bill from my hand. Living was cheap out here; I'd just bought her a week that would likely wind her up with another man in another county, far from Bitsy.

"Well," she said, "I tried. Nobody can say I didn't try."

I nodded, and she nodded back, finally. She slouched back to the El Camino. The car door groaned from the rust. I waited by the door until the car was just a dust devil out on the far edge of the world.

Then I turned. I walked to the back of the house and into the bedroom. Bitsy was on the bedspread, playing with some tin cowboys from a yard-sale outfit. Peg was lying on her side, expressionless.

"Gone," I said.

⌒

Peg comes back empty-handed. She's been gone for a while and she's begun to pull herself together, the hair brushed, the makeup reapplied. But the eyes are still old, brightness dimmed with the agony of the day, the lines furrowed with new knowledge.

The doctor comes tentatively, like a man who knows he is an imposter, a man who doesn't believe the diplomas hanging on his Sheetrock office wall.

"We tried to save the eye," he says, a vessel of apology. He endears himself to us by turning the culpability on himself. But it was me. I had been trying to fix the damned toaster when Bitsy wandered from my attention.

⌒

A few days after Dorothy left, Bitsy crawled across the woven rug, then stood against the chair, then pushed out into the room, unexpected and suddenly. Three good steps. On the couch, watching her, I realized something important was happening.

"Peg!" I shouted. "Come quick!"

Bitsy looked at me curiously and then plopped down on her ass. Peg came through the doorway from the hall, looking.

"Bitsy just got up and walked!" I said.

Peg looked at me, but she wasn't exactly happy. She looked at Bitsy sitting on the floor, then looked at me, then back at Bitsy.

"Bitsy walked," I said again.

Peg stood there like I was the problem. The moment was clearly over and Peg hadn't been there. Ever since that night I came back from finding Dorothy, Peg seemed insistent on doing everything Dorothy should have been doing. Bitsy sat staring, no movement toward trying to pick herself up again.

"Are you joking with me?" Peg said.

"Yeah," I said. "I'm just joking. Just pulling your leg."

"Well that's a little cruel, don't you think?"

"I guess."

"It is," she said. "Why do you need to go and be so cruel?"

Three weeks later, when Bitsy walked in Peg's presence, Peg seemed to be watching me more than Bitsy. I caught the glint of hard scrutiny without looking at her directly; I looked instead at Bitsy, who looked at me with what I swear, *I swear*, was guilt, and therefore complicity.

Peg is in the ladies' room when the doctor comes shuffling out, looking more grave and self-flagellating than before.

"Are you the grandpa?" he says.

"No," I say. I look down the hall to see if Peg's on her way back. "I'm not anybody—you know, in the family."

"I've got to get back in there," the doctor says. "Can I ask you to give the grandmother a message?"

"She'll be right on back."

"Can't I just tell you?" he says. "I have to, really, get back..."

His voice trails off and he looks trapped in an awkward

moment, and I turn and head down the hall, mumbling something about please waiting two seconds. At the ladies' room
door I swing it open and call inside: "Peg? Doctor needs to talk
to you . . ."

"*What?*" Her voice is clear, keening out from the stall. I hear
her fumbling with things and I recede to wait with the doctor.
In the hallway, she looks at me in exaggerated disbelief and then
turns her attention to the doctor.

"Well, there'll be quite a scar," he begins.

The day after Bitsy walked "for the first time," Peg decided
Dorothy should be made aware of this, to emphasize what a
bad mother she was being.

"Maybe it will shock her into straightening up, knowing
what all is passing her by," Peg said. "Maybe it will be a good
punch in that face."

So I went, again, looking. I rumbled through the soft night
marveling at the sky, like a glowing tower of colors, and listening
to sweet songs whistling through the AM radio. I went to all the
familiar places, searching. To tell Dorothy she didn't see Bitsy
walk for the very first time.

And in the familiar places I saw all the familiar faces, griz-
zled men leaning over their beer, part of the fraternity who might
have been Bitsy's father but wouldn't have any idea anyway.

"Seen Dorothy?"

"No, sir."

"Any you boys seen Dorothy?"

224 / EDWARD J. DELANEY

"Not so recent that she'd still be there."

I nodded and pondered. "Any you boys know where she's staying these days?"

All down the bar, Dorothy's men shook their heads.

⌐⌐

Bitsy isn't coming home tonight. The stitching is done but there's likely a concussion, and the doctor nervously describes how they'll look after her.

"She's as well as you can expect, after something like that," the doctor says. "You folks might as well get on home and rest. Wouldn't be comfortable, trying to spend the night."

It's a quarter to eleven. Peg walks across the parking lot to the truck with me following ten feet behind. I drive; she stares ahead. When we come through the kitchen door, into the dark house, the shards of broken dish crunch under my boots. I snap the overhead light on, get out the broom and the dustpan, and get to work. The lights are off in the living room. I can hear Peg, sitting on the couch crying.

⌐⌐

There was a shack behind a bigger house out on a forsaken ranch that hadn't been worked in years. I leaned into the iced gusts while I opened the gated barbed-wire, then jumped back into the truck and rumbled across the cattle grate and up the hill toward the hard place where the land edges to dishwater sky. Over the rise I could see the house and the smaller building, long since shifted out of square by the prevailing winds, hard wind out here that could make a man forget what it felt like to stand up straight. Remote country, fallow and neglected. I'd heard this was family property and that the owner, through inheritance, lived in Kansas City, trying to get by, and sitting on this place until someone was ready to make a foolish offer, or any offer. The house's windows were mainly broken. The shack, out fifty paces from the mudroom of the house, looked like nothing more than a tool shed, but I'd been told Dorothy might be staying at a farm, somewhere, they didn't know where. I'd already circled one after another, but this looked possible. She had no vehicle, and probably no money; her men kept her supplied, was what I'd heard. Her men who slipped her money while they tucked in their shirts. Still.

I rolled the truck down to the head of the rough double-track, where it bloomed into what was understood to be a parking area of hard dirt cut with tire tracks. I slipped the truck out of gear and gunned the engine enough to sound like the Second Coming. Anyone in that house was going to come out cursing, but no one did. I didn't much feel like getting out of the overheated cab, and the cold outside my frosted windshield was only part of that resistance.

I sat listening to the radio for a long time. The music was old-time, all the same heartbroken pining, less the electrical instruments. The singer put his destitution into cascading words, so good you wouldn't take him for a man long rich on his music. Some people just had the hurt inside them, regardless of the facts. Dorothy never had it harder than anybody else, but that wouldn't be her version of the story.

I reluctantly got out of the truck and coughed loudly, which couldn't nearly compete with the wind. I knew I'd end up knocking, but I shouted "Hello!" three times so I could say I did. Nothing. The shed had a loose brass knob and when I touched it the sensation is liking shaking hands with an ice cube. Then the door gave and I swung it in. The inside didn't give itself away by its temperature; it was flat cold and only less windy.

"Dorothy?" I shouted.

I let the eyes adjust. I could see the woodburning stove, gone cold, with the poker laid out on the floor in front of it. There was a good pile of quarter-split wood next to it; if I wondered, it was cut short when I saw Dorothy.

She was on the couch, the eyes looking at me even though the skin was as cold as the sky at my back. I knew if I touched her she'd be frozen, or close. She was in a bathrobe and her hair was wrapped in a towel. A bowl sat on the floor next to the couch, the scoured lines of the last bits of her meal rimming the inside. A tattered woman's magazine, probably out of a waiting room, was across her stomach. On the table over her shoulder, a candle was on a chipped dish, burned down to stub. She'd have died in a warm room that couldn't go on like that without her. Whatever got her was from inside, and my guess was the drugs more than the drinking.

I pulled the door shut and outside that little shack, I twisted and yanked at the knob until it came off in my hand, leaving only the square spindle sticking out of the hole. Out on the main road, I waited until I was far off, my wheels rolling out too many miles for anyone to make a connection. I tossed out the knob, which skittered and bounced until it jumped into the high grass down in a deep gully. There was no guilt in this at all. I'd learned how not to be noticed, how to make myself an ignored man. Keeping my mouth shut was the only way to keep on living the way I did. In that way, I could convince myself it was the right thing to do. Bitsy needed me. Somebody else could just as well find her, someone who could make the call without having to think about it.

⌒○

Now, home from the hospital, I don't turn on the lights. I sit on the couch next to Peg as she uses tissue to wipe the clumped mascara from around her tear-wet eyes.

"Bitsy will pretty much be okay," I say.

"Scarred," Peg says. "With a mother who couldn't give a damn either way."

Nobody's seen Dorothy in nearly a year. Months ago, Peg had taken a sick day and gone asking around, after I'd failed to turn anything up; one of Dorothy's men thought she might have headed for Houston. Peg, returning that night, had shaken her head in rueful but mild disgust that in one day she had turned up facts that I hadn't been able to determine in days of searching. The matter seemed closed, but I've spent this long stretch of time waiting for someone to surprise me with the news I already know. Every day for a few weeks after I stepped from that shed, I sat at the edge of every moment; then, for weeks, it seemed something would give. Finally, I left myself to the thought that maybe no one would venture out there for a long time, or that

228 / EDWARD J. DELANEY

there were men inclined to the same silence as my own, for whatever reasons. The more it went on, the more I heard Peg telling people how her no-account daughter had busted out to Houston with a baby in her dust, the more I thought of how bad it would be when it would have to be taken back. Yet it hasn't happened.

I sit on the couch in the dark, listening to Peg sniffle and settle. The sleep will come on her like a surprise, and that's the only reprieve I can be sure I've got. Bitsy will live a life defined by the deep crescent wedge across her domed forehead, and by the missing eye; that will be the way I remember how I had let Bitsy wander, and it will be a connection that triangulates us in ways I probably don't want to think about. I don't have anywhere to go, and I am old now.

"Well," Peg finally says. "Bitsy will be a terror when she gets home."

"I guess."

"She'll be trying to pull off that bandage, sure as hell."

"I know."

"We need to keep a closer watch over her," Peg says.

"Damn right we will."

"The damned toaster didn't even matter," she says quietly.

"I'll learn," I say.

Overlook

I remembered the city and how the outdoors of it was laid in narrow strips of open space worked into the eternal indoors. And I remembered that house in Wyoming, standing against the sky like a protrusion, something to enter by necessity, only when the world that was real drove you in with hail or the teeth of cold winds or sheets of rain. There was a place she liked to sit, and she called it "Overlook," like on a long highway where a blue sign suddenly denotes overlook, as if by decree, as if in ridiculously arbitrary selection. The house had windows but that was different. It was shelter but not a place to live. Out there was where you lived. I had wandered for so long, almost forgetting why I had left. It didn't matter after all, I guessed. After dinner, we'd have to go out, feel the cold, watch the sun bottom out. I could see her face growing old in the prairie wind. It always felt as if I had finally stopped.